THE GIRL IN THE TOWER

THE GIRL IN THE TOWER

LISA SCHROEDER

with illustrations by Nicoletta Ceccoli

Christy Ottaviano Books

Henry Holt and Company

New York

Henry Holt and Company, LLC
Publishers since 1866
175 Fifth Avenue
New York, New York 10010
mackids.com

Henry Holt® is a registered trademark of Henry Holt and Company, LLC.
Text copyright © 2016 by Lisa Schroeder
Illustrations copyright © 2016 by Nicoletta Ceccoli
All rights reserved.

Library of Congress Cataloging-in-Publication Data
Schroeder, Lisa.
The girl in the tower / Lisa Schroeder ; with illustrations by
Nicoletta Ceccoli.—First edition.
pages   cm
Summary: "An evil queen kidnaps ten-year-old Violet to turn her
into a princess"—Provided by publisher.
ISBN 978-0-8050-9513-5 (hardback)—ISBN 978-1-62779-493-0 (e-book)
[1. Fairy tales.   2. Kidnapping—Fiction.]   I. Title.
PZ8.S3126Gi 2016   [Fic]—dc23   2015003081

Our books may be purchased in bulk for promotional, educational, or
business use. Please contact your local bookseller or the Macmillan Corporate
and Premium Sales Department at (800) 221-7945 ext. 5442 or by
e-mail at MacmillanSpecialMarkets@macmillan.com.

Book design by Eileen Savage

First Edition—2016

Printed in the United States of America by R. R. Donnelley & Sons Company,
Harrisonburg, Virginia

1 3 5 7 9 10 8 6 4 2

*For the librarians of the world,
who bring joy and magic to the
lives of many.*

— L. S.

PART ONE

Locked Away

I

As Violet hovered in that reflective space be-tween asleep and awake, she reached up to feel for her nose. Thankfully, it was still there. Practi-cally numb, but there. She burrowed deeper under the blankets. Not quite ready to face another day in the dreary tower, she squeezed her eyelids shut. Per-haps she could delay the inevitable by drifting back to sleep and returning to the garden of her dreams.

There, sunshine warmed her through and through. There, she frolicked about and admired Mother Nature's handiwork with no walls to confine her. And there, the colorful hummingbirds never left her side.

Merciful sleep did not come, however. The young girl rolled over and squeezed in tightly against her mother underneath the old wool blankets they shared. Her delicate snore soothed Violet's frigid nerves. She fingered the soft leather bracelet she wore on her tiny wrist, and soon her own breaths matched those of her mother. Comfort filled her. As long as she had her mother, she could bear anything. Even the bitter cold.

A while later, her mother stirred and Violet's stomach growled. When had they last eaten? Yesterday? The day before? The cold made Violet's thoughts fuzzy, but surely Maggie hadn't forgotten them yesterday. She made a point to come every day, for she and her husband, George, were the only connection Violet and her mother had to the outside world. Maggie's visits were important, treasured even, and not just for the food.

"Are you hungry, my little princess?" her mother asked, rolling over and kissing her daughter's forehead.

"Aye. Starving," Violet replied. "What did we eat yesterday? I can't seem to recall."

"Boiled eggs. One in the morning and one in the evening."

Now Violet remembered. She detested boiled eggs. She must have pushed them from her mind, so unpleasant was the experience of having to choke them down.

"I do hope she brings something else today. Bread and freshly whipped butter. With fresh strawberries. And cream to drink."

"Strawberries don't grow in the winter, silly girl. You remember, don't you? They grow in early summer, when Lady Sunshine magically transforms the berries from green and paltry to red and plump."

Violet licked her cold, cracked lips. "And bursting with sweet flavor. Oh, Mama, what I would give for just one strawberry. Remember the first time I tasted one, from the plants George grew in the secret garden?"

Her mother sighed. "I do indeed. Good friends, George and Maggie have been—that's for sure. Risking so much to show us kindness. We're forever in their debt."

"Aye," Violet said, deep in thought, remembering warmer and happier days.

"Come on, now," her mother said, sitting up. "Let's not mope about. After all, we have a treasure to find today. Isn't that right?"

Violet sat up, too, a smile slowly spreading across her face. Just like that, the straw beneath them wasn't a mattress at all, but a ship sailing across the rolling waves of the ocean. "Have we almost reached land, Captain Nuri?"

"Ahoy, matey. See there? Land straight ahead!" Her mother pointed across the room. "It won't be long now. Do you have your treasure map?"

Violet reached toward the wall directly behind the mattress and pulled out a loose stone. Hidden away were a quill pen and ink, along with some parchment and a lovely book of artwork. Over the years, Maggie had smuggled various items into the tower for the two prisoners so Violet could learn to read and write and draw. Violet grabbed the treasure map she and her mother had drawn as they imagined an island with warm, sandy beaches and palm trees, and a chest filled with jewels waiting to be discovered.

"The sea is getting rough," Captain Nuri said. "Are you sure you are capable of landing this fine vessel?"

Violet handed her mother the map, then stood up on the mattress turned ship. She curled her fingers, making a small hole with each hand, and put them

together before she placed them over her right eye.
It was as if she were looking through a spyglass, just
like her mother had taught her. She was no longer
a girl shivering in a tower, but a pirate, strong and

brave, ready to fight battles and locate the buried treasure.

"Captain Nuri, I will have no trouble landing this ship. If I can survive all these years in this tower, I believe I can do anything!"

Nuri smiled proudly. "That's my girl."

2

While a mother and daughter searched for imaginary jewels in the cold, bleak tower, Queen Bogdana, wrapped in layers of fur, walked the castle grounds, searching for a different kind of jewel. A flying jewel.

The queen collected beautiful things the way historians collect books. She had trays of sparkling jewelry; closets of exquisite gowns and robes; and, her favorite of all, acres of gardens where flowers, plants, bushes, and trees grew, producing colorful and fragrant blooms most of the year.

Yes, Bogdana, who wasn't a queen at all but instead

an evil witch, was obsessed with beauty. The spells her mother and grandmother had taught her as a young girl provided almost everything she desired: a home and husband fit for a queen, hardworking servants, and riches beyond compare. But every morning for the past twenty years, since she'd cast a spell on the castle and made herself queen, she looked in the mirror with disdain. For there was one thing her heart longed for until it ached.

To be beautiful herself.

She wanted to be rid of the fat, snoutlike nose; the beady eyes; and the splotchy skin. Even her brown hair was coarse and wiry, sticking every which way so that her large, jeweled crown appeared to rest on a bed of dried weeds.

The ancient spell book was clear. Only one act of magic could bring about beauty, and it required two items Bogdana did not have. Yet. She needed a feather from a living hummingbird and a strand of

hair the color of darkness plucked from the head of a
girl with eyes the color of lavender who had lived at
least eleven years but no more than twelve.

All of Bogdana's magic came from spells passed

down through generations of witches. It frustrated her at times that she couldn't simply wish for something and make it so. How much easier her life would be, she often thought, if her magic wasn't confined to spells that were oftentimes complex.

Even where her magic was concerned, she was never quite satisfied.

She ordered soldiers to search the country far and wide for a girl the right age and with the appropriate features for the beauty spell. None was found.

And then, one spring day ten years ago, as a band of wandering minstrels made their way along the road in front of the castle, a woman cried out in pain. The king, a kind and gentle man who was under Queen Bogdana's spell, heard the commotion and took pity on the musician Nuri when he learned she was about to deliver her first child. He invited Nuri into the castle, where she could rest and labor in private. The remaining minstrels, including the woman's husband,

Marko, were asked to make their way to the nearby village, where they could wait for Nuri to return to them with a swaddled babe in her arms.

When the infant was born, Nuri named her Violet. The queen made a visit to pay her respects and was astonished to find Violet was the girl the queen had been looking for, though eleven years too soon. With dark hair like her mother's and eyes a lovely purplish-blue color, the babe was a sight to behold. The queen decided she must somehow keep the girl in her possession until she would prove to be useful.

Once the minstrel was strong enough to return to her roaming lifestyle, the king asked his wife to help Nuri get on her way toward the village, where her family waited. Instead, without the king's knowledge, the queen ordered her servants to lock the woman and her child away in the east tower with only a straw mattress to sleep on and a small table and chairs for their daily meal. Bogdana gave a tower key to Maggie, one of the castle's maidservants whom she trusted implicitly, with instructions to gather up clothing for them to wear and to do their laundry regularly. Maggie was also told to take food and drink to them once a day, empty their chamber pots, and have her husband, George, provide buckets of water for a weekly bath.

The queen's instructions about the imprisonment were clear: If Maggie, or anyone else, let Nuri or Violet out of the tower, the sentence would be death for all those involved.

With one part of the spell taken care of, the queen turned her attention to the hummingbirds, which weren't native to the land. She read books about the delicate birds with tiny feathers that hover over flowers, and the more she learned, the more she wanted not just a single feather, but an entire flock of the birds. For if many hummingbirds came to live near the castle, she would surely have magnificent gardens beyond compare.

Time and time again, men were sent across the sea on ships, with promises of bags of gold in return for the little birds. Time and time again, the men returned empty-handed, for the journey was long and rough, and feeding the birds sugar water and insects outside their natural habitat proved almost impossible.

Finally, after four years of multiple attempts, a miracle occurred. A handful of hummingbirds survived the difficult trip. They were released into the garden before the queen had a chance to see them. Bogdana was furious at the men, though they thought they'd done her a favor, getting the birds to natural food and water before they perished like the others.

"Tell me about them," she'd said. "Tell me what the birds are like."

"You can't even imagine how small they are," one of the sailors had told her. "Teeny-tiny things, with colors so bright they are surely precious like jewels."

"Flying jewels," the queen had whispered. "Exactly what my garden needs to make it the most beautiful in all the world."

Over the years, she'd had brief glimpses of the

birds, but only a few times. She longed to see one close-up—to see it hover above a plant or drink nectar from a flower. But most of all, she longed to hold a tiny feather in her hands, one step closer to the beauty she had dreamed about for so long.

"Where are you, my little birds?" she whispered now as she walked the path, her breath like a small cloud in the cold air. "You can't hide forever. Your beauty will be mine one day soon. Of this I am certain."

3

*T*ucked away directly behind the tower at the far east end of the castle was a small outdoor space surrounded on all four sides by a tall beech hedge. No one who lived or worked at the castle ever visited the spot, for it was rumored to have been an ancient burial place. Many believed that to disturb the holy ground would be to ask for a lifetime of misery, for the dead would surely haunt those who trespassed.

George, who had worked as the gardener at the castle since the witch had become queen, did not believe this superstition to be true, however. He had always thought it was sad to waste such perfectly good soil.

When his wife, Maggie, told him years ago of the woman and the child who had been banished to the tower, it occurred to him that he could turn the neglected space into something useful for the young girl. And so, despite the queen's wishes that the prisoners never leave the tower, George began the task of creating a secret garden for Violet. He wanted her to have

a place outside to call her own, where she could feel the sunshine on her skin, breathe in the fresh air, and experience the beauty of nature firsthand.

For years, in his spare time, after his regular gardening duties were performed, George cultivated the land behind the tower. Once the soil was nice and rich, he planted grass seed and small trees, flowers, and bushes.

The result was nothing less than astounding, and he wasn't the only one who thought so. The hummingbirds that had been brought across the ocean by ship made their way to the secret garden, where George had planted plenty of foxgloves and hollyhocks. He had hoped to lure butterflies to the garden, for Maggie had her heart set on seeing an indigo butterfly. The blue butterfly was extremely rare, but Maggie spoke of it often. Never in a hundred years did he imagine that Violet's garden would become home to some of the loveliest birds he'd ever seen.

When Violet came to visit the garden, as she did most days, it was more than a place to run free. It felt like she truly belonged, for the birds had taken to Violet as if she were one of their own.

As George walked along the garden path on a winter day, making note of the work that needed to be done, he recalled the first day Violet visited her special garden. It was so clear in his mind it was as if it were yesterday.

When he'd told Violet he had a big surprise for her fourth birthday and they would have to leave the tower to see what it was, her pretty eyes had grown big and round.

"Can Mama go, too?" she'd asked.

"Neh. It's not possible, lassie. The hole you'll use to get outside isn't large enough." He'd looked at Nuri with sympathy. "I'm sorry, love."

"'Tis fine. I've had a lifetime of sunshine and fresh air till now. Poor Violet has had only these horrid walls.

Just watch yourselves, please. The queen mustn't find her out there."

"She'll be perfectly safe," George assured Nuri. "The beech hedge around the perimeter will keep us hidden. And we'll be sure to speak softly."

After they said their good-byes, George took Violet down the long spiral staircase of the tower until they reached the bottom. On one side was a regular door, and on the other, a narrow loophole in the wall.

"That hole will take you to your surprise," he told his young friend. "As you can see, I can't fit through it, so I'll use the door and come around through a gap in the beech hedge to find you."

"But what's the hole really for, George?" Violet asked him.

"If we ever went to war, an archer could stand to the side of the hole and watch for enemies. If an enemy were to come into sight, he could simply move to the center of the hole and shoot with his bow and arrow."

Violet listened intently. As she began to ask something else, George gave her a gentle push and said, "Not now, darlin'. Just do as I say, and go through the hole. I'll be there in two shakes of a lamb's tail."

Once he emerged through the bushes, George found the four-year-old standing smack-dab in the middle of the square space, looking straight up, as one of her hands tried to shade her sensitive eyes from the sun. He turned his head to the sky as well and watched as cotton-like clouds moved ever so slowly. *What a sight the vast blue sky must be to someone who's been confined to a small, simple room*, he thought.

It struck George in that moment how truly small Violet was. He and Maggie had discussed the girl's size, blaming her tiny frame on the lack of sunshine and proper nutrition, for the cook was not generous in the food he prepared for the prisoners. But as he saw her there, in a large, open space, her size really came to light.

When Violet's eyes had adjusted to the brightness

of the outdoors, she walked all around the garden, looking at the flowers, touching them gently, as if they might disappear at any moment. When a bee buzzed near her, she didn't run, like most children would, but instead smiled and reached her hand out and said, "Hello. I'm Violet. Who are you?"

With George's help that day, the young girl learned about insects as they studied dragonflies, butterflies, spiders, and bees. She also learned the names of the flowers: lilies, dahlias, cosmos, hollyhocks, and many more.

George recalled it was the hummingbirds that'd really won her over, however. She'd spotted two of them, floating among the bright pink foxgloves, and she watched in awe as one hovered in midair, drinking the nectar from a bloom through its beak.

"What are they?" she'd asked, her eyes the color of joy.

"Hummingbirds," he'd told her.

"The hummingbirds are like me," she'd said, flapping her arms and running around the garden. "They are small, but they can do amazing things. I might be small, but I can be a pirate or a princess or an artist. I can do amazing things, too. We are alike, the birds and me." She'd flapped her arms harder, pretending to fly. "George, we are the same. Don't you see?"

He'd smiled. "I do indeed."

OVER THE YEARS, it was quite remarkable how close the birds and the child had become. They were truly the best of friends. Violet could stand in the middle of the garden with her hands extended, and the birds would land on her, resting peacefully while she spoke softly to them.

Once, just recently, two birds with brilliant green, blue, and gold feathers had landed on Violet's thin bracelet, the one Nuri used to wear. George had overheard the child speak to the birds.

"How nice," she'd whispered. "You are fond of the bracelet, as am I. My mother gave it to me so I could feel close to my papa, for he wears one exactly like it. My greatest wish is that someday he, Mama, and I shall be together. If only I could fly away from this place with you. You are so lucky to be free."

THE WINTER MONTHS were hard on Violet, for the hummingbirds flew south to find warmer temperatures. Like every year since Violet had first met the birds, George, Maggie, and Nuri would help her through the upcoming gloomy season as best they could. She loved playing imaginary games, hearing stories, looking through the art book Maggie had given her, and drawing. They'd keep her as busy as possible.

George shook his head, stopped walking, and looked around. He told himself to quit daydreaming, for he had work to do. Very soon he needed to gather the buckets of water and take them to the tower so Nuri and Violet could bathe. Maggie was probably there now, delivering their breakfast.

It would be difficult to see Violet today, George thought, for he knew they had probably seen the last of the birds yesterday, and he needed to give her this news. He should have told her to say good-bye until spring, but he hadn't had the heart.

Lost in his thoughts once again, he didn't see Queen Bogdana coming down the pathway. All of a sudden, she was there, standing in front of him, covered in furs. He couldn't help but think how unfair it was that she had so much while Nuri and Violet had so very little.

"Good morning, Queen," he said as he bowed.

"I am extremely disappointed I haven't seen my precious birds for so long," the queen told him. "Have you spotted them recently?"

He pointed to a simple sparrow in the tree. "Why, yes, Your Highness. There are plenty of birds in your garden. I wonder, is your eyesight starting to fail?"

She scowled at George. "You fool, my eyesight is fine. I don't want to see *those* birds. I want to see the hummingbirds that cost me a fortune. So I ask you again: Have you seen the dainty birds with colorful feathers?"

Of course he had, but he'd seen them only in the secret garden. To tell her about them would be to give up Violet's joyous place and get them all in trouble.

"My apologies," George said. "I haven't seen any hummingbirds in your garden. They must keep themselves very well hidden. But now that the cold temperatures have arrived, I'm afraid they have probably migrated south for the winter. Might be best to wait and look for them in the spring."

Queen Bogdana glared at him. George thought he saw a hint of suspicion in her eyes, but he could only hope he was wrong.

"If I must wait, I shall," she said, practically snarling. "But next spring, if the birds don't appear, there will be grave consequences." She looked at the tower in the distance. "There are two prisoners I have been more than kind to. I've put a roof over their heads and have fed them daily for ten years! But I assure you, if I do not get what I want, I will be kind no more."

George swallowed hard. "What are you saying, exactly?"

"I'm saying," she bellowed, "the girl and her mother will die!" And with that, she turned and stormed toward the castle.

4

*T*he birds that had traveled a great distance on a ship to a new land had lived a glorious life in the small garden behind the tower. But it wasn't the many flowering plants that made it so.

It was the small girl who visited almost daily.

They appreciated her joy and her exuberance for life, but most of all, they treasured the way she looked at them—as if she understood them completely and would like nothing better than to be one of them.

On the ship, the birds had seen the eyes of greed in the men who had hunted them.

The few times they'd ventured out into the main

garden, the birds had seen the eyes of vanity and self-ishness in the queen who longed to own them.

But in the girl, all they saw was understanding, appreciation, and unconditional love.

As new birds were born and old birds left this earth, love for the girl was passed down, generation to generation. And each new generation of birds was greeted by Violet, who spoke kindly to them, pretended to fly with them, and simply adored them.

It was now winter, and most of the birds had begun their migration to a warmer climate. However, two hummingbirds, Peace and Pax, both with brilliant green, blue, and golden feathers, had stayed behind. They were especially close to Violet, and they didn't want to go quite yet. It pained them to think of leaving the girl without any birds to keep her company when she ventured outside.

It was for that reason that they heard the threat that bleak winter day, when the queen's loud, sharp words shot across the grounds and into the small garden behind the tower.

"The girl and her mother will die!"

They didn't know if anyone else had heard.

They didn't know if anyone else cared.

But they had heard. And they cared. Very deeply.

They believed a child's life depended on them. Never had two creatures felt so impossibly small.

5

*G*ood morning to you," Maggie called as she un-
locked the door of the tower and entered.

Violet jumped from her pretend ship. "Good morning, Maggie!" She longed to know what they'd be having
for breakfast today, but her mother had taught her at an
early age to never ask. Maggie was first and foremost
their friend.

"A tad chilly this morning, eh?" Maggie asked. "Are
you two holding up all right?"

"We're just fine," Nuri said as she stood. "Please
don't worry about us."

"I've got a surprise for both of you this morning,"

Maggie said. "Two bowls of steaming-hot porridge. With honey!"

"Glory be!" Violet cried. "Thank you for not bringing stinky old eggs again."

"Violet!" Nuri said. "You know better than to complain about Maggie's delivery for us. Go sit in the corner until I call you to eat."

Violet started to protest but stopped, for she knew it was no use. After ten years, she'd never seen her mother back down from a punishment, not once. So she went to the corner and sulked.

Maggie handed the tray to Nuri, who began setting the food on the table while Maggie carried the chamber pots outside.

"I hope the porridge helps warm you," Maggie said upon her return. "I begged the cook to give you some. I told George last night, I don't know how you two have survived living in this drafty old tower so long. Haven't got much of anything, the two of you, but you sure do have a hefty dose of determination. More so than I'd have, I do believe."

"Well, what choice do we have, really?" Nuri said. "We must hold on until Marko comes back for us."

"But it's been so long, love," Maggie said softly.

"He'll come for us," Nuri said strongly. "He won't stop looking until he finds us. There is nothing he wouldn't do for me."

"Like when he saved you from the horrible thief on the beach all those years ago, before I was born?" Violet called from the corner.

Nuri smiled. "Yes, my dear. Exactly like that. Please come and eat your delicious porridge now. And apologize to Maggie."

Violet scurried to the table. "I'm sorry, Mama and Maggie. I will try my best not to complain about the food, including stinky eggs."

Nuri stroked her daughter's head of wavy, long black hair. "Thank you. Now let's enjoy our breakfast. Eat every drop, for it won't do us any good later."

"I don't believe I've heard the story of the thief," Maggie said. "Did he carry a weapon?"

"Yes!" Violet said before Nuri had a chance to respond. "He snuck up behind them, grabbed Mama, and held a knife to her throat. The thief demanded that Papa give him the pouch of coins hanging from his belt."

"Oh dear," Maggie said, looking at Nuri. "What in heaven's name did you do?"

Violet took a bite of the warm porridge. It was the best thing she'd tasted in a long time. "Go ahead, Mama. Tell her what happened."

"Well," Nuri said, "I think we were aware that simply handing over the money might mean a death sentence for both of us. After all, why should he leave behind witnesses to his crime? But my husband, he's a clever fellow. He held the pouch out in front of him and told the man to reach and get it. As the thief went to grab for it, he let go of me, and I ducked away as Marko threw the pouch into the ocean. While the thief ran off to retrieve the coins, we escaped unharmed."

Violet watched her mother's face as she remembered that day. Somehow she managed to look happy and sad, all at the same time. Violet knew it was because her mama loved her papa very much and liked remembering him, but she missed him terribly.

"When you returned to your musical family," Violet

said, wanting to finish the story the proper way, "Papa told them what happened. And then you leaned over, kissed him on the cheek, and said, 'You are my hero, and I love you.'"

Violet's mother smiled. "That I did." She took a deep breath and looked at Maggie. "And I am certain he will be a hero again. It is the hope I hold on to, like a treasured tambourine, that keeps me going day after day."

The three sat in silence, lost in their thoughts, until there was a knock at the door.

"That will be George," Maggie said as she went to answer it. "He said he'd be bringing you some bath-water today."

As Maggie let her husband into the tower, Violet finished the last bite of her porridge and sprang from her seat. "George, I'm happy you're here. May we go and see the birds later this afternoon? After I've had my bath and found the buried treasure?"

"Well, good morning to you, too!" He carried two buckets in and dumped the water into the round wooden tub. "The water shouldn't be too cold, since the buckets sat by the fire all night long. Now, let me get the rest, and then we'll talk about the birds, eh?"

Violet nodded. "Aye."

When he'd finally finished his work, he turned and knelt down, opening his arms wide. Violet ran into them, happy to get a hug from the man who had given her so much.

"Did I hear you mention a buried treasure?" he asked Violet as she stepped back. "Must be a pirate in the tower today. Am I right?"

"Yes, that's me! We have a map, and soon we'll reach land so I can begin searching for the gold and coins."

"That's wonderful, darlin'." He stood up and turned to Nuri as he stroked his crimson beard. "It's colder than the dickens. Is there anything at all I can do for you?"

Nuri stood. "It's cold—that's for sure. But we're fine. We've got each other, after all."

"Can we go this afternoon, George?" Violet asked. "To the garden, to see the birds? Can we? Please?"

George knelt down again and took Violet's tiny hands in his rough and callused ones. "Violet, it pains me to tell you this, but I doubt we'll see any birds today."

Violet didn't have to ask, for she knew what this meant. Still, she asked anyway, just to be sure. "Have they gone for the winter?"

"I believe so. But like every year, they'll be back in the spring, lassie, before your birthday's here. They love you too much to stay away any longer than they have to."

She threw her arms around his broad shoulders, blinking back tears. "I will miss them."

He stroked her hair and whispered in her ear. "I know you will. And they will miss you, too." When she finally pulled away, George said, "Now, about that treasure hunt. What do you say we have one in the garden? I will make you a map and give you a hand spade for digging, and you can find something special that I hide in a secret spot."

Violet clapped her hands together. "Really? You'll do that for me?"

"I will indeed. Of course, I shall need some time to prepare. I know you are anxious, but I think tomorrow would be best for a treasure hunt. Can you wait, pirate Violet?"

"Aye!" She hopped around on one of her small legs, filled with excitement. "It will be such fun, I know it will be worth the wait."

George stood up and put his hands into his coat pockets. "Why, I almost forgot." He smiled as he pulled out a cloth and proceeded to unwrap it. "I snuck something from the kitchen this morning while the cook wasn't looking. Cinnamon cookies. Baked just yesterday."

Nuri walked over and took the treats from George, as Violet stopped hopping and licked her lips. "How kind," Nuri said. "I think we'll save them for after the bath."

"Thank you," Violet said, the delicious smell of cinnamon hanging in the air. "Cookies make me almost as happy as hummingbirds."

"I reckon I knew that," George said.

Violet and Nuri said good-bye to George and Maggie, who had to get back to their duties, and thanked them again for their kindness.

"All right, my little princess," Nuri said once they were alone. "Get undressed and jump into the bath. I'll go after you."

As Violet slipped her clothes off, she said, "Mother, it's not a bath—it's the ocean. And I am a mermaid, like the picture in the art book. I will swim around in the sea and sing songs to the sailors."

"What song shall you sing?"

"You shall teach me a new one. Something you sang with my papa. Please?"

Her mother didn't sing often. She said the music of her people made her miss them deeply. But once in a while, Violet was able to talk her mother into it.

"I suppose I could sing for you today," her mother said. "How about this one?"

And with that, Nuri began to sing, her voice prettier than any songbird Violet had ever heard.

We don't know where we're going,
only know where we have been.
The road we're on is called Freedom,
and we'll walk it again and again.

She continued on, verse after verse. The song spoke of a wandering life and the love of family, and Violet felt so happy she wished she could climb inside the music and live there.

"Again. Please?" Violet said when Nuri's voice went silent. "I want to learn it and sing it with you."

Her mother gave a scrap of soap to Violet before she began the song again. And for the next long while, they sang and splashed as the little mermaid swam in the deep blue sea.

6

*T*he band of wandering minstrels had been known far and wide for the music they played. In every place they stopped to perform, the village buzzed with excitement right up until showtime.

Marko had played the lute, while Nuri had played the tambourine. The two had grown up together in the caravan, their parents the best of friends. When Marko had asked for Nuri's hand in marriage at the age of twenty and she'd accepted, he'd believed they had many wonderful years to look forward to.

And then, one warm spring day, the dreams he'd had for a happy life were snatched away. At first it seemed almost like a miracle, Nuri giving birth inside the castle. Marko knew she would be well cared for, given food, drink, and a bed to rest upon until she felt strong enough to return to them. But as the days dragged on, it felt like a curse more than a blessing.

In the nearby village, the minstrels talked of the newborn, placing bets as to whether it would be a boy or a girl. And they waited. They talked of Nuri and what a good mother she would be. And they waited. They remembered happier days, when Nuri and Marko were children, splashing along the shore, and they spoke of returning there with a new child.

It was agonizing to wait, but wait they did.

After many days and nights, the moon turned from round and bright to just a thin sliver in the sky, and Marko could bear it no more.

"It has been too long," Nuri's husband told his family and friends. "Something is not right. She should have been here by now."

"We shall go for her," Nuri's father said.

"All of us?" Marko asked. "Is that such a good idea?"

"There is strength in numbers. We shall all go."

When they arrived, the guards who stood at the gate told the minstrel group there was neither a commoner nor her infant anywhere in the castle.

"Please, let me speak to the king," Marko begged. "He's the one who invited her inside. Perhaps he knows where she is."

They pleaded their case, assuring the guards she had indeed been there, and all they wanted was to be reunited with her and the child once again.

Finally, one of the guards agreed to speak to the king and see if he had any information for them.

The king was surprised to hear the news of the missing woman and agreed to go and tell the group what he knew. When he appeared in front of them, wearing a robe of velvet around his shoulders and magnificent gemstone rings on his fingers, the minstrels bowed. The king was a handsome man, with golden locks of hair framing his face and kind green eyes. Again Marko was struck by how trustworthy he looked. That was why he'd agreed to the arrangement and let his wife go into the castle without him.

"The woman you are seeking went on her way," the king told them. "Many days ago. If she did not return to you, perhaps she wanted a different life for her and her daughter. I'm very sorry, but there is nothing I can do. She is gone."

"A daughter," Marko exclaimed, taking in the bittersweet news. "I have a daughter. But where in the world is she?"

"I do not know," the king said. "You have my sympathies."

The king sounded genuine. Besides, Marko thought, what reason did he have to lie? There was nothing to do but go and search for the missing woman and child.

For years and years, the minstrels looked, but they didn't find a single clue. It was as if Nuri and the infant had vanished from the face of the earth.

One spring morning, nine years after Nuri had gone missing, Marko awoke and realized they were camped just a few miles from the castle. He decided to return there alone to see if he could gather any additional information about his wife. Though it was a horrible thought, it was possible the king hadn't told the truth that day long ago.

Marko didn't tell a soul where he was going. He

snuck out of camp before anyone was awake. When he arrived at the castle, only one guard was at the gate. Even better, the guard, who had perhaps been on duty through the night, was asleep. Quiet as a rabbit, Marko tiptoed by the guard, and then, once safely past, he ran, as fast as he could, toward the far side of the castle, hoping to find a servant's entrance he could use to get inside. He thought he might try to find a maid or someone else to talk to who had been in the castle the day his daughter was born.

As he made his way through the expansive garden, he stopped when he saw three hummingbirds hovering above a large honeysuckle bush with pink blossoms. They shimmered in the early-morning sunlight. Marko held his breath, not wanting to frighten them, completely captivated by them.

"Do you know where my wife and daughter are?" he whispered. "They have been gone for so long. I'm here to find them."

They quickly fluttered away, and then, a moment later, a voice boomed from behind him.

"Were those my flying jewels?"

He turned to find a hideous woman standing in front of him.

"Is that what you call them?"

"That's the first time I've seen them," she said. "I wasn't sure they still lived." She looked at the man. "What business do you have in my garden?"

"Your garden, ma'am?" he asked.

"Yes. I am the queen of this castle."

Marko bowed, his heart beating rapidly. "I apologize, Your Majesty. I didn't realize it was you."

"So tell me: Who are you, and why are you here?"

He stood up, tall and proud. "I am here seeking answers about my wife and daughter. Nuri gave birth in your castle nine years ago, and I have not seen her since. We have inquired at every village known to us, and no one has seen her. Would you be so kind as to tell me if you know anything about their where-abouts?"

The queen's eyes shot a dagger toward the man. "Indeed. I know exactly where they are. Your wife and daughter are locked in the tower at the east end of the castle. And they will remain there until I say otherwise."

Marko dropped to his knees, took the queen's hand, and kissed it. "Please, I beg you, show mercy and release them. They have done nothing to deserve such a harsh punishment. I will give you everything I have. Everything I own. 'Tis not much, but it is yours."

As he stood, Marko released a leather pouch from his belt and handed it to the queen. She opened it, turned it over, and dumped the coins onto the ground. Then she rushed about, collecting items from the garden and throwing them into the pouch—the web of a spider, a handful of clover, bark from a sycamore tree, and dandelion seeds. When finished, she plucked an eyelash from her left eye and threw that in as well.

"What are you doing?" Marko asked.

She raised her hand and sprinkled the ingredients she had gathered onto the man's shoulder, while chanting:

Colors bright, clear your sight.
You shall walk away with might,
never looking back this way—
your memory is erased today.
Only the feather of a hummingbird
will free your mind, grant your wish,
and let the love of your heart be heard.

Marko felt dizzy. He closed his eyes for a moment, hoping to steady himself. When he opened them, he felt...different. He looked at his surroundings, and nothing was familiar. Furthermore, he was completely alone.

"Where am I?" he whispered.

On the ground, by his feet, coins were scattered, as if someone had dropped them. He gathered them up, wishing he had a pouch to make carrying them easier.

His stomach growled.

I must find the nearest market, he thought.

And with that, he turned and made his way down to the road.

A year and a half later, he was still wandering alone, searching for something. And, oh, how he wished he knew what it was he was looking for.

7

*T*he two birds that had stayed behind while the others flew away did not want to leave their friend. But they knew they had to go if they wanted to try to save her life. The girl who came from the tower, who spoke to them with such kindness and love, needed to finally be set free.

So Peace and Pax flew.

They flew away from the bitter-cold winds and the garden they loved, toward the warmth of the sun.

They flew farther than they'd ever flown before, to a place where the air felt clean and fresh, where flowers grew alongside the road, making it easy to find nourishment as they traveled.

The little birds watched as people passed by, for they knew only one person could truly help the girl—the man she'd spoken of the day Peace and Pax had

landed on her pretty bracelet. The man they'd seen one day in the castle's garden, before the queen had approached and frightened them away.

They remembered the girl's words. It was her greatest wish that she and her father be together. Now the two tiny birds intended to do whatever it might take to make her wish come true.

8

*A*s the afternoon sun shone through the one and only window in the tower, providing much-needed warmth, Violet sat at the table with the art book, a piece of parchment, and the pen and ink. Her mother sat beside her, sewing scraps of fabric together to make a dress for Violet. Maggie secretly saved scraps for Nuri, who very much enjoyed making clothes for her daughter.

"I am drawing a field full of flowers," Violet told her mother, "underneath a clear blue sky. It is sunny and pleasant, and I'm calling it the perfect place for hummingbirds."

"Ah," Violet's mother said as she sewed another stitch. "Very nice."

"It keeps them safe and warm all through the winter, until it is time to return here to me. Because my secret garden is the other perfect place for them." She looked at her mother. "I wonder, Mama, where is your perfect place?"

She reached out and touched her daughter's cheek. "Why, that's an easy question. Wherever you are."

"Even here, in this miserable tower?"

"It's not a miserable tower now, Violet," she said. "It's a studio, where a famous artist studies from a lovely book and creates artwork that will soon be adored the world over."

Violet sat up straighter. "I am famous?" she asked.

"Certainly," her mother replied. "If only we had some glue, we might hang all your lovely artwork on the walls for display. But no matter. People are still gathering outside, hoping to get a glimpse of your latest masterpiece."

"I wish those imaginary people were my sweet, lovely birds," Violet said. "Then I would be overjoyed."

Her mother laughed. "Always thinking of the birds, eh?"

Violet looked at her mother. "Are you sad you've never seen them?"

"I suppose now and then I'm disappointed I can't go to the garden with you. But you are always so thoughtful, bringing me dahlias and lilies and other pretty flowers."

"I'm sorry I can't bring the birds to you," Violet said. "But I draw you pictures of them."

"Indeed you do."

"Do you think Papa would enjoy my artwork?"

"Oh, yes, I know he would. He would enjoy everything about you, love."

Violet looked at her mother then, afraid, as always, to ask the question she'd thought about for so long. But she couldn't hold it in any longer. "Why hasn't he stormed the castle and come for us by now?"

Nuri took a deep breath and set her sewing on the table. "Sadly, that is a question I don't have an answer for. Perhaps he has tried. Or maybe he has been waiting, patiently, for the right opportunity. Whatever it is, we mustn't doubt him."

"I hope something hasn't happened to him," Violet said. She quickly picked up her pen and began drawing again.

"I'm sure he is fine," her mother said. "We mustn't worry, for it does us no good."

"Look what I've done," Violet said, pushing the paper toward her mother. "I've drawn him here, in the field with the birds. He will be safe there, too. And soon my little friends will lead him to us, and we will finally be a happy family."

"I like the way you think," Nuri replied as she returned to her sewing.

"One day, when we leave here, will I become a minstrel, too?" Violet asked.

"Yes, of course, for you are one of us."

"But I don't know how to play an instrument."

"Your papa and grandpapa will teach you."

"Sometimes I try to imagine what it must be like," Violet said. "To travel and see new places every day. To meet people. To be…free." She looked at her mother. "You don't speak about it much. About missing everything you had before coming here. Perhaps because you don't want me to see you sad. But you do miss it, don't you?"

Her mother stared at the picture on the table. "I cannot lie, Violet. I do miss it. The world is a magical place, and there is so much to see. And freedom, well, it is a glorious thing I took for granted. And when we leave here someday, trust me, I will appreciate every free minute we have."

"Me too," Violet said. "May I take another piece of parchment? I'd like to draw one more picture."

"Of course. What shall you draw this time?"

"A picture of you, Papa, and me," she said, getting up from her chair, "smiling because we are so thankful to be free."

9

With their duties finished for the day, George and Maggie met up, as they did every evening, to walk to their hovel, a simple hut, on the far west side of the castle grounds.

"I had a conversation with the queen earlier," George told Maggie as they strolled beneath the shimmering moon, the faint smell of manure and hay in the air from the nearby stable.

"About what?" Maggie asked, taking George's arm.

"She's none too happy with the hummingbirds. Said if she doesn't see them in the spring, there will be grave consequences for Nuri and Violet."

"What do the two of 'em have to do with the queen seeing the birds?"

"I don't have a clue," George said.

"Does she think you can control where the birds spend their time?"

"Appears so," he replied as they approached the hovel.

"You don't think she knows about the secret garden, do you?"

He opened the door for his wife. "I believe if she knew about Violet's garden, she would have told me. Still, I got the feeling she wonders if I might be keeping secrets from her."

"How will you make the birds live in the queen's garden instead of Violet's?"

George scowled. "As I consider my options, I don't like the one that seems most likely to be the solution."

"And what is that?" she asked.

"I'm afraid the only way the birds will live in the main garden is if the secret garden is destroyed before their return."

His wife let out a small gasp. "But Violet—"

"I know, Maggie. Believe me, I know."

IO

The next day was a bit warmer, and Violet played on her pretend ship most of the morning, until George came for her in the early afternoon.

"Are you ready, pirate Violet?" he asked after he let himself in with Maggie's key.

"Yes, sir," Violet said as she skipped over to greet him. "Is the treasure hidden well and good?"

"Indeed it is," George replied.

"Tell me what it is I'm looking for," she said as she pulled on his arm. "Please?"

He laughed. "Now, where is the fun in that? No, you shall have to search for your treasure and discover what it is, like a real pirate."

"I can't wait to see what you find," her mother said, coming over to give her a kiss good-bye.

"Whatever it is, I shall be happy to share it with you, Captain."

"The kindest pirate I've ever seen," George remarked.

"That she is," Nuri said. "Have a great time!"

"We will," Violet said. "See you soon."

Down the staircase the two went, and when they reached the loophole and the door, they went their separate ways, like always. When George came through the hedge, he held a map in one hand and a small gardening tool in the other.

"Here you go, lass," he said, handing the items to Violet. He looked at something on the ground and his brow furrowed. "Ah, criminy."

"What is it?" Violet asked.

"I forgot to clear away a large limb that fell onto the garden pathway. Queen will have my hide if she comes across it."

"Go," Violet said. "Do your work while I search for my treasure. I'll be fine here by myself. I'll stay quiet and won't set foot outside this garden. Mark my word."

"Are you certain?"

"Yes, I am. Please, go so you don't get in trouble."

"All right. I'll be back as soon as I can."

Violet smiled. "I know you will."

Once he'd gone, she opened the map, her heart racing. After being confined to the tower all day yesterday, it felt good to be outside, in her favorite place, having an adventure.

She licked her lips as she studied the map. George had drawn it as if the garden were an island, with ocean waves all around it, and a large ship tied near the shore. There were three small trees in the garden, and George had drawn them in their rightful places.

She counted the dashes and began walking. One, two, three... When she reached twelve, the dotted line took a hard right and went eight paces that way, and then two paces back down. She stood on the edge of the flowerbed now. An X marked a spot on the map. Was she in the right place?

The only way to find out was to start digging, so that was exactly what she did.

II

Queen Bogdana had gone to the kitchen in the wee hours of the morning, when no kitchen staff were around to see her there. She made potions only in private, for although she had cast many spells throughout the years, no one knew the queen's true identity.

Her magic was extremely powerful—recipients couldn't recall the spell being cast or that Bogdana had done anything remotely witchlike. From deep in their soul, the recipients would have a longing for the item that would break the spell, if it was possible, but they wouldn't know why they had such a longing. Because of the inability to remember what had been done to them, spells were rarely broken, and as far as Bogdana was concerned, that was exactly as it should be.

Now the truth serum she'd cooked up according to the ancient spell book's recipe was in a goblet, ready to be consumed. From her bedchamber, Bogdana sent one of her servants to fetch Maggie, ordering her to come at once.

When Maggie came into the room, her eyes filled with concern. "Your Majesty, I came as quick as I could. What may I do for you?"

The queen picked up the goblet and took it to Maggie. "Drink this. Does it taste strange to you? I'm concerned we may have a bad batch in the cellar."

"But, Queen, I am only a maidservant. I do not know the particulars of—"

"Taste it!" the queen bellowed.

With a shaking hand, Maggie reached for the cup. Bogdana watched as she raised the potion to her lips.

Once Maggie had swallowed a time or two, grimacing as she did, the queen spoke the incantation quickly.

Sun and moon, save help me now,
I seek the truth here not yet found.
For one full day, no less, no more,
facts be spoken, my powers implore.

Queen Bogdana grabbed the goblet before Maggie let it drop from her hands. The maidservant blinked a few times, swaying back and forth, as if she had trouble staying upright.

"Come and sit," the queen said, taking Maggie's elbow and guiding her to a chair.

"Oh, my heavens," Maggie said a minute later, looking around before her eyes landed on the queen. "Whatever happened? And why am I in your bedchamber, Queen?"

"I called you here," she replied, "so that I might ask you something. And now I have no doubts that you will speak the truth. Tell me, Maggie: What do you know of the hummingbirds? You are married to the gardener, and I believe he's keeping secrets from me. Tell me the reasons why I don't see the special birds in my garden more often."

Maggie's eyes glazed over, and the way she spoke, it was as if someone else had taken hold of her body. "The hummingbirds live in the secret garden. They have lived there since they arrived on the ship all those years ago. The girl who lives in the tower visits them daily. My husband says Violet and the birds are kindred spirits. They love each other. They are both small, yet they shine with beauty and light."

The queen paced the floor, seething with anger, as she pondered what the maidservant had just told her.

A secret garden?

That was where her precious birds lived?

And the girl visited them *daily*?

"I should have you both murdered," the queen hissed, "for betraying my orders and letting the girl out of the tower. Tell me more about this secret garden. Whose idea was it, and where is it, exactly?"

"The secret garden is behind the east tower," Maggie replied. "It is the spot rumored to be an ancient burial place. My husband did not believe the superstitions, and so he planted grass, shrubs, flowers, and a few trees. George is the one who created the garden for the girl. It is a lovely place, and I'm sure you would enjoy it very much, Your Majesty."

"Yes," she muttered, pacing again. "I'm sure I would."

"As a matter of fact, my husband is there right this moment," Maggie said. "He is with the girl, playing a game."

At those words, it was as if someone had put a hand out and stopped a spinning wheel from turning. The whirlwind of thoughts in Bogdana's mind became only one: *I must go see the secret garden for myself.*

"You may go," the queen told Maggie. "Return to your duties."

Maggie stood and bowed her head. "Yes, my queen."

Once the maidservant had left, Bogdana collected her thoughts. She didn't have a moment to lose if she wanted to catch George and the girl in the garden.

He had disobeyed the queen. And she intended to make him pay.

12

*B*unches of wild columbines along the road provided Peace and Pax with plenty of nectar for their ever-hungry stomachs. As they drank their fill, they heard music in the distance. They turned to see a group of minstrels coming toward them, walking alongside a colorful house on wheels pulled by two horses. The birds listened to the words of the song.

We don't know where we're going,
only know where we have been.
The road we're on is called Freedom,
and we'll walk it again and again.

They sounded happy, yet sad. Like the last days of summer, when the sun is warm and the garden is filled with color, yet change is on the horizon.

Every day we meet new people,
singing songs to bring them joy.
Our hearts miss Marko and Nuri,
but our faith shall not be destroyed.

The birds enjoyed the music. It spoke to their tiny hearts, and it was familiar. It reminded them a bit of the times the girl spoke in the garden.

And so they followed the minstrels, humming along, the way hummingbirds do.

13

*V*iolet pulled the wooden figurines out of the pouch, one by one, completely enamored with the treasure she'd found. There were five of them in all, and they were magnificent. George must have spent hours carving them. Surely he hadn't done it all yesterday. Perhaps he had been working on them for a while and had decided this would be a fun way to surprise her, Violet thought.

However he had managed to do it, she was thrilled with the gift.

Three of the figures were people, and Violet knew George had made them with her in mind. One was a girl holding a sword, one was a girl wearing a robe and a crown, and the last was a girl with a bird in the palm of her hand. Over the years, George had seen her as a pirate sailing on the ocean, a princess with a wool blanket as a robe, and of course, the girl in the garden who talked to the birds.

He had also made two beautiful carvings of hummingbirds. She held a bird in one hand and pirate Violet in the other, and returned the rest of the carvings to the pouch, which she set beneath a tree. With her arms above her head, she held the figurines in the air as she ran, as if pirate Violet had wings and could fly alongside the bird.

"You there!" A booming voice came from behind Violet, making her freeze. "Stop that nonsense and come this way."

Violet slowly turned around, fear instantly replacing the joy she had felt just a moment before.

Never had she been this afraid.

Never had she felt so alone.

Violet hesitantly took a step and then another toward the woman at the other end of the garden. Who was it? she wondered. She clutched the figurines tightly in her hands and began wishing.

Please let her be kind.

Please let her be a friend to me.

Please let George return so he can help me if she is not.

"Come, now," the woman yelled. "Quickly. Don't you know when the queen gives you an order, you must obey?"

A chill ran through Violet's body, from the top of her head to the tips of her toes. After all, it was because of the queen that Violet had lived ten years and had yet to meet her father.

The girl wanted to turn and run far, far away. But of course, she had nowhere to go. She had no choice. She had to do as the queen said.

Once Violet stood in front of the queen, it was a

long time before anything was said, as the queen looked her up and down.

"You are a beautiful girl," she finally said. "More beautiful than I ever imagined."

"Thank you," Violet replied softly, her eyes focused on a leaf on the ground. The queen made her extremely uncomfortable, but it wasn't just that. The queen was so ugly it was difficult for Violet to look at her. She hadn't even known a person could be that hideous.

"Where is the gardener?" the queen asked.

"He is attending to his duties. He shall be back shortly."

"Is that right?" She turned her eyes away from Violet and looked around at the garden. "So this is where my flying jewels live?"

Violet looked up. "Flying jewels? You mean the hummingbirds?"

"Yes. Where are they?"

"They're not here. Flown south to find warmer weather. But they shall be back in time for my birthday."

The queen raised her eyebrows. "Is that so? That is the birthday when you shall turn eleven years old, yes?"

"Aye."

"What a wonderful day that will be," the queen said with an evil smile as she imagined the moment when beauty would finally be hers. "Now, tell me: Is it true the birds are quite fond of you?"

"'Tis true," Violet said. "And I of them. Mama says we are kindred spirits."

"Your mother, she stays in the tower when you come down to the garden?" the queen asked.

"She must stay there," Violet said, wishing now more than ever that weren't the case. "She can't fit through the hole I use to get from there to here."

It seemed to Violet that she should perhaps apologize for leaving the tower. After all, George had told her many times she must be quiet in the secret garden. To be discovered, he'd told her, would mean terrible things for Violet and her mother. Violet did not want terrible things to happen to them.

"I beg your pardon," Violet said meekly. "I will return to the tower and stay there until you say otherwise, if that is what you wish."

"No," the queen said as she stroked her chin, looking off into the distance. "As I stand here and think about all this, I do not wish for that at all."

"Is George in trouble?" Violet asked.

"Yes," the queen said matter-of-factly.

"Am I in trouble?"

"Actually," the queen said with a gleam in her eye, "this might be the luckiest day of your life."

14

*T*he two hummingbirds followed the wandering minstrels all the way to the coastal village of Armanie, where the misty sea air reached up to greet them. Peace and Pax had never seen the ocean before. It seemed to stretch on forever.

The birds stayed back, admiring the ocean from afar, for no flowers seemed to grow in the gritty tan dirt that lay at the feet of the sea.

After the minstrels frolicked in the water, they headed toward the marketplace, wearing the sea with their smiles and singing the sweet but sad song once again.

They hadn't gone far when one of them called out,

"Is that him?" More yelling ensued, and the birds became frightened. They had never heard the minstrels yell before.

Peace and Pax stayed back, waiting and watching, hovering in an azalea bush, hoping the minstrels would be all right, for they had become fond of them.

And then a man appeared, and the minstrels laughed and patted him on the back and gave him hugs and kisses. The birds flew closer. They wanted to see this man who made everyone smile.

The crowd grew quiet, forming a circle around the man. He looked afraid. Confused. "I do not recognize you," he said. "Who are you?"

"We are your family," an older man replied. "We've been looking for you. One day you left camp, and you never returned to us."

"I'm sorry," the man said. "I'm not sure of what you speak."

The minstrels buzzed with conversation.

"Shhhh," the old man hissed. "Quiet! Marko, you really do not remember us?"

The frightened man shook his head.

And then he slowly backed away, holding his hand up, a thin leather bracelet sliding ever so slightly down his arm.

15

*I*t definitely was not the luckiest day of Violet's life. When the queen told the girl she would be going back to the castle to live as a princess, Violet's first thought was of Nuri.

"May my mother come, too?" Violet asked.

"No," the queen said. "She may not. She is a wandering minstrel. She doesn't belong in a castle. But you. You are young enough to train. You really have two choices, as I see it. Come with me to live as a princess and obey me as a daughter would, and I shall set your mother free. Refuse, and you will both be thrown in the dungeon, where you will beg for death to take you."

"Tell me about the dungeon," Violet said, wanting to consider her choices carefully. "How is it worse than the tower we've lived in all this time?"

The queen scowled at the girl. "It is dark and damp, and it smells of death. Rats dwell there. Have you ever seen a rat, Violet? I suppose you haven't. They are disgusting creatures, with sharp teeth and long tails, and they will eat just about anything, including a small girl's fingers and toes. And if I still haven't convinced you, please consider that there would be no kind maidservant to bring you daily food and drink. You'd be lucky to get garbage scraps once every few days."

Violet gulped. "And what would it be like to live in the castle?"

"Ah, now, here is where it is all good news. You shall have your own room, with a down mattress and a fire burning in the hearth. You shall be given the finest clothes to wear and the very best books money can buy for your studies. Servants will wait on you hand

and foot. Once you are crowned, the staff shall call you Princess, and a fine princess you will be!"

One question haunted Violet's thoughts. "Why?" she asked the queen. "Why would you do this for me now?"

"That is a fair question," the queen replied. "First of all, I have always dreamt of a beautiful daughter like yourself. I am unable to have children. Second, I want to know the hummingbirds as you do. When they return in the spring, you shall introduce them to me. What a splendid time we will have with the birds in the garden, you and I, together. There won't be a person alive who does not envy us."

Violet looked up at the tower, trying to imagine a life without her mother. It was like trying to imagine a world without the sun and the moon. Impossible. Tears filled Violet's lavender eyes.

"Are you certain there are no other choices?" Violet asked in a very small voice.

"Positively certain. Now, come along. I've stood out here in this frigid garden long enough. Let's go, and I shall show you to your new room."

"May I please say good-bye to my mother?" She sniffled. "Please, Your Majesty? And then I will go with you as you wish."

The queen reached down and grabbed the child's hand, forcing the wooden carving of the bird from her hand. "No. It is time we go. I assure you, it is for the best, for seeing her again would prolong your pain. The sooner you can begin to forget about your mother, the better. Mark my word, your mother will be a carefree minstrel once again, very soon. Each of you shall have the best of both worlds. Don't you see?"

Free, Violet thought. *My mother shall finally be free.*

It was this thought, and this thought alone, that allowed Violet to maintain her composure as she walked alongside the queen. Violet still held the pirate carving in her other hand. If the queen had seen it, she hadn't made mention of it. Violet slipped the small statue into her pocket. The queen might have taken everything else, but Violet wasn't about to let her have that one last possession.

The carving would be a reminder of the happy times Violet had spent with her mother. Perhaps they'd had their share of difficult times, as all pirates do, but they

had survived. Not only that, they'd had loads of fun doing it.

The sea is getting rough!

Never had the words been so true, even if there wasn't a drop of water in sight.

Don't worry, Captain Nuri, Violet thought. *I will be brave and strong. Just like you.*

16

When George entered the garden and didn't see Violet, he thought perhaps she was hiding.

He called to her softly as he searched behind trees and bushes. "Violet, come out, come out, wherever you are. I want to hear what you think of your gift. A talented fellow must have made it for you, eh?"

When she didn't respond, he went to the place where the treasure had been buried. The hole was empty, telling him the satchel had been found. As his eyes took in the surrounding area, they landed on the item a short distance away, near a tree. He went to it and picked it up. When he peered inside, he noticed two of the carvings were missing.

She must have taken them to show her mother, he thought.

He ran to the tower door and took the steps up two at a time. When he reached the door that led to Nuri and Violet's home, a wave of disappointment washed over him. How foolish of him. Violet couldn't have come up to show her mother, for she didn't have the key.

Agony gripped him as he debated what to do next. If he went through the door without Violet, Nuri would surely ask where her daughter was, and, of course, he wouldn't have an answer. But shouldn't she be told that the child had gone missing? Nuri was her mother, after all.

He decided he would look a bit more before he talked to Nuri about the situation. If he found Violet, as he hoped he would, he'd save Nuri a great deal of worry. And if he didn't, well, he'd cross that bridge when he came to it.

Upon checking the secret garden one more time, he stepped on something hard in the grass. When he reached down to see what it was, he found one of the carved birds. It was as if she had dropped it there by accident.

The bird went into the satchel with the other figurines. George's heart was growing heavier by the minute. He told himself he must keep looking and, more important, must hold out hope that he would find her.

Perhaps she had gone looking for him, he thought. Or perhaps the wooden carvings had made her miss the birds and she'd gone to look for them. With that in mind, he left for the main garden.

He searched for a long time, but there was no sign of her. Not even so much as a clue. While he walked toward the castle to get Maggie, he remembered the words Violet had spoken before he'd left her.

I'll stay quiet and won't set foot outside this garden. Mark my word.

He felt ill as panic spread through his body like a burning fire.

Someone had taken Violet from her private garden.

But who?

And why?

17

*T*he tower was extremely quiet when Violet wasn't there to chatter away about this or that. It seemed to Nuri there was an endless supply of Violet's curiosity, which was a good thing, most of the time. Like anything, too much and it could grow tiring.

As much as she loved her daughter, Nuri found the brief period of silence while Violet visited the garden a welcome relief. It allowed her time to think about the past, the present, and the future in a way she couldn't when Violet was there, interrupting her every thought. She often used the time to consider helpful lessons for her daughter.

Nuri knew it was important to teach Violet as much as she could with the few resources she had. Over the years, she'd made it a point to teach her how to read and write, how to speak properly, and how to count. She also tried to show her as much of the world as she could by reading books Maggie would sneak in from time to time.

It was Nuri's greatest hope that someday they would leave the tower, and she didn't want her daughter to be a stranger to the ways of the world. Every day, she kept that thought in mind as she tried to teach Violet as much as she was able.

The day of the treasure hunt, Nuri sat down and tried to focus on creating some new astronomy lessons. But for some reason, she couldn't focus. She felt anxious, and it bothered her, for, as far as she knew, she had no reason to feel that way.

She found herself staring at the artwork Violet had created the day before, thinking of her husband

and feeling sad that he had missed out on so much of their daughter's life. He would be proud of Violet. She knew that for sure. The child had grown up with so little, and yet she was kind, inquisitive, and smart.

Nuri picked up her sewing project, hoping it might help to settle her nerves. And it did, for a short while. But when Violet didn't return from the secret garden, Nuri's anxiety returned. She paced the floor, back and forth, back and forth, wondering what was taking so long.

Finally, after hours had passed and she was practically sick with worry, Nuri heard the familiar click of the key in the lock. She ran to the door, and when it flew open, she looked down, expecting to see Violet's smiling face.

But that was not what she saw. Not even close.

Nuri's eyes quickly traveled up until they met the queen's.

"Where is she?" Nuri asked, trying to peer behind the queen's large frame.

The queen pushed past Nuri and into the small room, the door slamming behind her. "You've disobeyed me. All of you."

"What have you done with her?" Nuri asked. "Bring her to me. Now."

Bogdana turned and glared at Nuri. "You best watch your tone. Your fate, as well as your daughter's, lies in my hands."

The queen took in the small room. She stared at the pictures Violet had drawn. Nuri silently kicked herself for not hiding them. She and Violet had been so careful all these years, making sure to put smuggled goods away in the secret hole when they weren't being used. Although the queen had never visited them until now, Nuri had always been aware that she could, at any time.

"The child did this?" the queen asked as she went

to the table and picked up one of the drawings. "She's quite talented. And surely you must know I never gave permission for you to have such extravagances as parchment and ink."

Nuri didn't respond, hoping the queen would let it slide. The less she said about George and Maggie, the better.

Queen Bogdana set the picture back on the table and went to the window. The sun was starting to set, turning the sky into a playground of pastels. Nuri thought of all the times she'd stood there with her daughter, watching the sun disappear as day turned to night. Neither of them liked nighttime much because of the darkness it delivered. But never, Nuri thought, had it been as dark as this moment. Never in her life had she been so frightened.

Nuri dropped to her knees and clasped her hands together. "Please, Your Majesty. Tell me what to do to get my daughter back. Whatever it is you want, I shall do."

The queen turned around. "You must know that

your daughter's beauty is magnificent," she said. "The way her dark hair contrasts with her light lilac eyes, she is a sight to behold."

"Indeed," Nuri said. "It is true."

"Though she is quite small."

Nuri rose to her feet. "That is the reason I let her play outside. She needed the sunshine and fresh air, as all children do. Surely you can understand."

"As I said, you disobeyed me. And I assure you, I plan to make you pay for your disobedience."

"Do what you will to me," Nuri said, bowing her head. "But I beg you to take mercy on my daughter, for she has done nothing wrong."

"I hear she is quite good with the flying jewels. Is it true they will fly right up to her?"

"The hummingbirds? It is indeed true, for they adore Violet."

"Once they return in the spring," the queen said, "I expect her to teach me everything she knows about them."

When she heard the queen speak of the future, hope ignited in Nuri. Perhaps Queen Bogdana wasn't as coldhearted as Nuri had thought. The queen would let them live. It seemed Violet would have to spend time with the wicked queen, teaching her about the birds, but it would be a small price to pay.

"I'm sure she would be happy to instruct you on whatever it is you'd like to know," Nuri said. "She's a very agreeable child."

"Agreeable is good," the queen said. "For there will be many new things she must grow accustomed to in the coming days."

Nuri did not like the sound of this. "Whatever do you mean?"

The queen moved toward the door. "Right now, your daughter is taking a rose water bath. Tonight she will sleep on a down mattress in a room with a fire burning the whole night through. In the coming days, she will have the finest clothes, the finest food, and the finest books for her studies."

Nuri's jaw dropped open as she took in the queen's words. She remembered the way Violet had looked when she'd left the tower, wearing a skirt Nuri had made for her along with a blouse and an old rag of a coat, hand-me-downs provided by Maggie. She re-membered how cold Violet had been yesterday morning. And how hungry she'd been, with only two boiled eggs to eat. Was it true what the queen said? Was it all coming to an end for her daughter?

"You are letting her live with you?" Nuri asked. "For how long?"

"Listen closely," the queen said, "for this will be the last time I speak of this matter with you. I intend to make Violet a princess. She will become my daughter, for she has beauty beyond compare and knowledge of the birds I long to possess. We will be a pretty and powerful pair, with flying jewels by our sides wherever we go. Together, we will become the most admired people in all the land."

Nuri pressed her hand to her chest, for it hurt to hear the queen's words. It was clear the queen didn't want to be a mother to Violet. She simply wanted to use her to get closer to the birds, and to show her off, like a silver collection on display.

"I...I don't understand. She doesn't need you to be her mother. She has me."

"You are her mother no more," the queen roared. "Tomorrow you shall leave here, never to return. Never! If you do, I shall throw both of you in the dungeon, where nothing but death awaits you. If your daughter is to live, it *must* be without you."

And so, with those simple words, Nuri understood. There really was no choice. She had to let her daughter go.

"I'll have Maggie see to it that you are on your way tomorrow," the queen said. "I would send her now, but she and George are enjoying the company of the rats in the dungeon for the night. They certainly deserve harsher punishment, but I need their services, and so it will have to do. You can thank your lucky stars I'm not throwing you down there with them. Though I imagine spending this night alone will be far worse than any punishment I could think up for you."

Nuri bowed her head as tears streamed down her cheeks. It was so very true. "Yes, Your Majesty."

In the blink of an eye, the queen was gone.

And Nuri was left to endure the painful silence for the rest of the long, cold night.

PART TWO

Riches Await

18

Once inside the castle, the queen led Violet down numerous long hallways, up a flight of stairs, through a huge room with tall ceilings where servants were setting large tables, and up another flight of stairs.

Violet couldn't help but be amazed. The castle was truly magnificent, from the stained-glass windows that graced some of the rooms to the exquisite tapestries hung on many walls. Never had the girl who'd spent all her life in a tower imagined a place as grand as this castle.

They kept walking, down another long corridor and finally into a warm room filled with golden sunlight. The first thing she noticed was the bed. Oh, what a bed! It was enormous. From the top of the posts hung sheer white fabric. She couldn't help but notice all the wonderful windows. Her eyes landed on one at the far end of the room with a cushioned bench beneath it.

The fabric on the bench wasn't like anything Violet had ever seen. It was smooth and shiny and deep, deep red, the color of an overly ripe strawberry. She wondered what you could see from the window.

Ever so slowly, she walked into the room. Three wooden steps were at the foot of the bed, and Violet couldn't resist. She wanted to climb up and touch the beautiful bed with its luxurious bedclothes. It looked so lush, so inviting.

Just as her foot was about to take a step, the queen yelled, "No! Stop!"

Violet turned to face her, feeling very foolish. "I beg your pardon," she said. "I thought this room was for me. But now I see I am mistaken. A small girl such as

myself does not need a room this extravagant. Is this where you sleep, Your Majesty?"

The queen scowled at Violet. "No, this is not where I sleep. This is, indeed, your room. But you mustn't crawl on the bed until you've been scrubbed from head to toe."

"But I bathed just yesterday," Violet replied.

"That may be true," the queen said as she eyed the girl disapprovingly, "but you shall bathe again. With lots of soap and rose petals in the water. When you are finished, we will dress you in some proper clothes. Clothes fit for a girl about to become a princess."

At the word *princess,* Violet felt tears sting her eyes again, for it reminded her of her mother. She wondered, would her mother have used the pet name if she'd known this would be Violet's fate someday?

"Wait here," the queen said. "I must let the servants know of your arrival. Not to mention the king."

"Will he approve?" Violet asked before the queen turned to leave.

"Of course he will."

"What shall you tell him about me?"

She paused by the doorway. "That I found you wandering alongside the road, with no one to care for you and nowhere to go. I will say you are alone because of a tragic family accident, and it is only right that we take you in. There's no need to fret, for he will do as I say and agree to make you princess."

"So you will lie," Violet said. "Will you feel guilty, bending the truth like that?"

The queen waved her hand in the air, as if to dismiss the silly question. "I do whatever it takes to get what I want."

Those words sent a chill down Violet's spine. Something about the way she said it sounded so sinister.

"May I sit by the window while I wait for my bath?" Violet asked.

"I suppose. I must tell them to work quickly. The sooner you are cleaned up, the better. And do understand, I expect you to behave in my absence. I have important matters to attend to, so I will not see you again this day."

"Yes, Your Highness. You do not have to worry. I shall do as I'm told."

"Good." She smiled. "Aren't we off to a pleasant start?"

Violet did her best to smile back, but she knew it was a sad little smile. Yes, the castle was grand, but in her mind, there wasn't anything pleasant about all that had happened in the past couple of hours. It was the longest she'd been away from her mother in her entire life. How she wished her mother were here.

"Until tomorrow, then," the queen said before she left the room.

As soon as she was alone, Violet took the figurine out of her pocket and tucked it into the blankets of her bed. She wondered if George would find the others she had left behind in the secret garden. Perhaps he would bring them to her later, though she decided she'd rather he not, for she didn't want him to risk getting into any further trouble.

Hopefully, if he found them, he would give them to her mother before she was set free. That way, she, too, would have something concrete to remind her of the special times the two of them had enjoyed together in the tower.

Violet took a seat on the plush red cushion and finally let the tears fall. After all, she told herself, no one, not even pirates, can be brave and strong all the time.

19

Nuri opened one eye at the sound of the key turning in the lock. But she didn't move. Although she had lain in bed since the day before, after the queen had given her the awful news, she felt exhausted.

"Shall we wake her?" George whispered.

"I don't know," Maggie said. "I can't imagine she slept much last night."

With a heavy sigh, Nuri opened both eyes. It wasn't right to let her friends bumble around, unsure how to proceed. As much as she might wish she could stay in bed and wish the world away, she knew it was time to face the new day.

Once she sat up, Maggie came rushing over to pull her into her arms. "I'm so very sorry, love."

Nuri held back the tears, for it would do no good to make her two friends feel worse than they already did. As Maggie helped Nuri to her feet, Nuri asked, "How are you two holding up, after all you've been through?"

"Don't worry about us," George said, setting some baskets and a jug on the table. "'Twas a long night, but we're fine. 'Tis you we're concerned with now." He looked at the floor, shame covering his face. "I must apologize, Nuri, for I believe this nightmare is all my fault. I shouldn't have left her alone, even for a second."

"Please don't blame yourself," Nuri told him. "We're all responsible in one way or another. After all, we knew we were taking a chance by letting her leave this tower, and we all believed sunshine and fresh air for Violet was worth the risk."

"I want to assure you I'll look out for her," Maggie said.

"Thank you," Nuri said, walking to the table to pour herself something to drink. "That comforts me."

"You mustn't give up hope," George said sternly. "Perhaps a time will come when you can be reunited with your daughter."

"Where will you go?" Maggie asked. "Do you think you can find your husband?"

Nuri shook her head. "I'm not sure. Part of me wants to search for him, while the other part wants to stay right here. I'm afraid if I leave, I'll have lost my daughter forever."

George frowned. "Well, you certainly can't stay. And you wouldn't really want to, would you?"

"What if the queen didn't know I'd stayed on? You could tell her I'd left, and she'd most likely never check to see if it were true. Do they have someone else to put up here in this horrid place?"

Maggie and George looked at her like she'd lost her mind. "Nuri, freedom is yours now. You must make the most of it. Go find your husband and get re-acquainted with him. You've missed him, haven't you?"

"Very much. But who knows where he is or how

long it'd take to find him? And I don't have any money. How could I survive on my own without a coin to my name?"

Maggie walked over to one of the baskets they'd brought. She reached in and pulled out a tambourine.

"We were going to surprise Violet for her eleventh birthday in the spring. But it seems like you can put it to good use."

Nuri took the instrument from her friend. She slapped it against the palm of her hand a few times, and the sound delighted her. It'd been a long time since she'd heard it.

"Oh, heavens. This must've cost you a month's worth of wages."

"You go on out into the world and make glorious music," George said. "And here are a few coins to hold you over until you can earn some yourself." He slipped a pouch into her hand. "Surely people will pay to listen to you sing and play. And then you'll find your husband, and you'll have your life back again."

Nuri bowed her head. "It's not a life without Violet."

Maggie rubbed Nuri's back. "It shall be difficult, I know. But you have to try." Maggie looked at George. "I was thinking, perhaps we could find a way to keep Nuri apprised of the situation here at the castle."

George was quiet for a moment, then his eyes lit up. "Yes. Of course we can. Nuri, there's a man at the market, an older man with a white beard and a mustache, who sells vegetables. His name is Richard, and he's a friend of ours. We can pass along messages for you through him. And if a time comes when we feel it is safe for you to return, we shall let you know." He reached out and squeezed Nuri's hand. "Cling tightly to hope, just as you have in the past, my dear. Evil can't rule forever. I truly believe that."

Nuri nodded, relieved that she would stay in touch with George and Maggie.

"One thing at a time," Maggie said. "Find your husband. Two heads are always better than one."

"Aye," Nuri said. "I suppose you're right."

"Before we go, I have something else for you," George said as he handed Nuri the satchel he'd been holding. "This was Violet's treasure. The one I buried in the garden? She left it behind. Well, most of it, that is."

Nuri took it from George and opened it up. "Oh my," she whispered. "George, these are wonderful."

She looked at each one carefully. Tears filled her eyes as she realized that two of the figurines were modeled after Violet. When she came to the princess one, she tried to laugh. "Who knew one day she'd actually become a real princess?"

"I carved one of her as a pirate as well," George explained. "That's the one I believe she somehow managed to take with her to the castle."

Nuri wiped a tear from her cheek. "Good. It will remind her to be strong and brave."

George put his arm around his wife's shoulders. "We best be getting back. Let's say our good-byes now, eh?"

They each took a turn giving Nuri a hug and a kiss on the cheek. Nuri would miss them desperately, as they had been such good friends. It comforted her deeply to know they'd be around to keep an eye on her daughter.

"Give Violet my love," Nuri said. "She is the song in my heart."

Maggie nodded. "Good-bye, dear."

And then they were gone, leaving the tower door wide open.

Nuri looked around the room she'd lived in for so long. How could she leave it and face the future with so much uncertainty? She'd never been alone before. She'd always had her family by her side, and then, after being ripped apart from them, she'd had her daughter. *Do I even know how to be alone?* she wondered.

Her hand still gripped the tambourine. She hit it against her thigh a couple of times and hummed a song that came from a distant memory. She thought of her family, a long line of musicians, always performing, in good times and bad. Could she learn to play while carrying around grief for all she had lost? She'd have to try. One thing was certain: She needed the earnings it would bring. And wouldn't Violet want her mother to play, so she could find her papa? And hopefully someday, they could find a way to get Violet back.

Nuri remembered Maggie's words. *One thing at a time.*

She took a deep breath and peeked into the basket of food they'd brought for her. Thankfully, it contained enough bread and jerky to last her a couple of days. In the other basket they'd left, she packed the tambourine, the satchel of wooden carvings, Violet's last drawings, and the smallest of the wool blankets. It was tight, but everything fit.

As Nuri turned to leave, she caught a glimpse of the half-finished dress she'd been working on the day before. She had an urge to take it with her, but she told herself it'd be foolish to do so. There wasn't room in the basket, and besides, now that Violet was living in the castle, she'd have no need for a patchwork dress made of rags.

The thought made Nuri both happy and sad at the

same time. The mixed feelings continued as she stepped out the doorway of the tower. At last, freedom was hers. And yet, until she was reunited with her daughter and husband, she had nothing to celebrate.

She couldn't help but smile as she remembered pirate Violet's words.

If I can survive all these years in this tower, I believe I can do anything!

Nuri told herself to hold tightly to that thought.

20

*A*fter a great deal of persuasion, the man wearing the bracelet joined the minstrels, and Peace and Pax watched as he became reacquainted with them. Night after night, the group would gather on the gritty tan floor next to the sea, build a large fire, and tell stories.

The birds couldn't get close enough to hear the stories, but they knew that the stories and the people telling them helped the man, for every day his eyes got clearer and his face looked happier.

One morning, while the rest of the minstrels slept, the man walked up to the road and past the firebush with many red blooms, where the birds were feeding.

"Flying jewels," he said when he saw them. "But wait. How do I know this?" He seemed to be concentrating hard, trying to gather the information from somewhere. Finally, he shook his head. "There is much I can't remember. Still, I know that's the name some use when speaking of you. And I must say, it fits. You truly are lovely, like jewels."

He reached over and fingered the bracelet on his wrist. "I long to have my memory back. They tell me my wife's name is Nuri. They say she disappeared years ago, after giving birth to our daughter. One day soon, they wish to return to the castle, for they suspect foul play. But what if we find my wife and daughter? How do I explain my inability to remember my marriage? It would be terrible to hurt a woman who has been through so much."

Of course, the birds couldn't answer him. They could only listen, as good hummingbirds do. The man stood there, watching the birds for a moment, before he turned and continued on with his walk.

Peace and Pax were pleased to hear of the minstrels' desire to return to the castle. As far as they knew, the girl and her mother were still trapped in the tower, and they wanted nothing more than to give the two their freedom. The small birds would return to the castle with the minstrels. And along the way, they would ask friends to join them, in case they were needed in the coming days and weeks.

You see, the birds knew that the queen might have a powerful husband. She might also have hundreds of soldiers at her disposal. She might even have magical spells.

But the queen did not have everything.

For she did not have flying friends in every field.

And she most certainly did not have love.

21

When Maggie walked into Violet's bedchamber, carrying various garments, Violet squealed and ran to her. "Oh, Maggie," she said, reaching out and rubbing the maidservant's arm. "It is so good to see you."

Maggie set the clothing down on the bed and turned to give the girl a hug. "Aye. And I'm glad to see you, too. How was your first night in the castle? Did you sleep well?"

Violet turned to the glowing fire that burned across from where she stood, its flames flickering this way and that. At long last, the ache she'd felt deep in her bones from being cold for so long was no longer there.

Between the fire and the comfortable bed, she should have slept soundly, and yet she hadn't. All night, she'd dreamt of her mother, and her dreams hadn't been happy ones. They were nightmares that made her sit up, trying to catch her breath, for no matter how far she ran or how hard she looked, she couldn't find her mother in the maze of the dark and frightening castle her mind had conjured while she slept.

"It was fine, I suppose," Violet replied, not wanting to worry Maggie.

"You can tell me the truth, love," Maggie said. "I know you miss her."

Violet gave her a small smile. "How do you know? Can you see it on my face?"

"It is only natural for you to be sad about being apart from your mother."

"Aye," Violet said.

"Now, I've come to give you a bath and get you dressed, so you may eat in the great hall today."

"A servant prepared my bath last night. The queen

must think I'm filthy, if she's having me bathe yet again."

Maggie chuckled as she helped the girl out of her nightdress. "I believe she wants to make sure you look your best for your introduction today. We'll wash your hair, and then I shall braid it for you. After today, you won't need to bathe again for a while."

"Should I be nervous?" Violet asked. "About the introduction?"

"No," Maggie said. "Not at all. Smile and simply be yourself."

Once undressed, Violet stepped into the silver tub with rose petals floating atop the warm water. She felt the heat from the fire on her bare back, and it was so different from the times she'd bathed in the tower, shivering most of the way through. Her mother had always tried to make it bearable, however, by telling stories or playing games.

At the thought of her mother, Violet felt tears rising up, but she told herself not to cry. If her mother could see her now, she would be pleased that her daughter was surrounded by such pretty things and so well cared for.

"Will Mama be all right?" Violet asked, blinking quickly so the tears wouldn't have a chance to escape.

Maggie took a sponge and began to scrub Violet's back. "Your mother will be fine. George and I took her a tambourine. We hope she will play music and use the money she earns to go in search of your papa."

Violet nodded. She relaxed and sank a little deeper into the warm water. "They will be happy minstrels again, wandering the countryside together. Just like before."

"Indeed," Maggie said.

"And I will be here, living the life of a princess. Like the queen wants." She felt a little tug on her heart as she said those words. Everything was better than she'd imagined, and yet, without her mother by her side, would she ever be truly happy? She knew she must try. As hard as it would be, she must try.

After all, her mother was free, just as she should be. Violet's new life was surely a small price to pay for that.

"Will I become a princess right away?" Violet asked Maggie.

"I have heard talk that they will crown you princess at a royal ball they shall give in your honor."

"What is a royal ball?"

"Hold your breath," Maggie said. She then dunked Violet underwater to get her face and hair wet. When Violet came back up, Maggie went to work lathering her hair. "A royal ball is a dance. People come from far and wide, dressed in their finest attire, and they hold a big party in the ballroom."

"But, Maggie, I do not know the first thing about dancing," she said as she wiped her dripping hair out of her eyes.

"Of course you don't, dear. And the queen is aware of that fact. I suspect the coming days and weeks will be busy ones for you. There is much she'll want to teach you before the big event. A princess plays a very important role."

Violet's voice was quiet. She suddenly felt teensy-tiny. "I'm scared. What if I disappoint everyone?"

Maggie leaned back and smiled. "You won't, love. Just do your very best—that is all they expect. You shall make a fine princess. Now, hold your breath again."

She did as she was asked so Maggie could rinse the soap out of her hair. This time, when Violet popped up, she kept quiet as she tried to imagine a big room full of people dressed up in fancy clothes, dancing.

What would her mother think of such a thing?

Violet turned her head and caught a tiny glimmer of something shiny hidden underneath a cloth in the corner. She hadn't noticed it the night before, for the sun had gone down and she'd bathed in candlelight.

"What is that?" Violet asked, sitting up straight, craning her neck to see.

Maggie turned to see what the child was looking at.

"Oh yes. That is a harp. Delivered a few days ago, as a matter of fact. A gift to the royal couple, though I'm not sure who sent it. They receive gifts often. The queen wasn't sure where to put it. Perhaps you'd like to try to play it?"

"Play it? A harp is a toy, then?" Violet asked as she stood up. Maggie helped her out of the tub and dried her off before she slipped a dressing gown onto the girl.

Maggie laughed. "No, not a toy, lass. A musical instrument. You strum the strings and it makes music."

Music. Violet had an instrument in her room that could play music! This wonderful surprise surpassed the soft bed, the lovely clothes, and the warm fire.

Violet went to pick it up, but she discovered it was quite heavy. She threw the cloth back and admired how lovely it looked.

"How do you hold it?" Violet asked.

"Take a seat on the bench by the window, and I'll show you."

Violet did as she was told and watched as Maggie

sat next to her and placed the harp in her lap. Maggie leaned the instrument against her chest and stretched her arms out on either side of it, strumming her fingers along one side and then the other.

Violet reached over and plucked a few strings.

"It is the music of my happy dreams," Violet whispered. "When I am outside with the birds, in the garden, this is the music I hear." Violet closed her eyes and imagined playing the harp outside.

"Lovely, eh?" Maggie replied.

"How do you know how to play?" Violet asked. "Did someone teach you?"

Maggie narrowed her brow and thought about the question for a moment before she finally responded. "It must sound strange, but I do not know the answer to that question. I cannot recall, exactly." She shook her head before she continued. "No matter. 'Tis not mine to play anyway."

Maggie then positioned the harp in Violet's lap. "Can someone teach me how to play?" Violet asked. "Please?"

Maggie smiled at the girl. "Perhaps. I shall see what I can do."

As Violet strummed the harp again and again, she thought of her mother, and what she might say if she knew Violet had her very own musical instrument to play.

Most likely something along the lines of, *Enjoy, my dear princess. Enjoy.*

22

I am not sure I understand why you must make her princess," the king told the queen as they discussed the matter in the privacy of the library.

The night before, the queen had told him the story she'd concocted about finding the young girl, and he had believed her. When she'd asked him what he thought of calling the girl their own and crowning her princess, he said he needed time to think about it. Now the queen was pressing him on the matter, for in a short while, they would all gather for the midday meal in the great hall. Violet needed to be introduced, and the queen wanted a decision on what they would tell everyone.

"This way, we choose an heir," Queen Bogdana asked. "Would you rather a cousin we hardly know take the throne instead one day? The girl is quite an agreeable child, as you shall see, and her beauty is beyond measure."

"Beauty is not a requirement of the throne," the king said. "Surely you of all people must know that."

The queen scowled. "No, it is not a requirement, but it is helpful. People will admire her. Respect her. Look up to her. Honestly, she will bring some much-needed joy to this castle, Your Grouchiness." She waved her hand. "Enough of this nonsense. She will become princess, and that is that. Unless you have a legitimate reason why we shouldn't go forward with it, you will make the announcement today."

"And you are certain Violet is truly an orphan?"

"Of course I am sure," the queen said, rising from her chair. "Now, if you don't mind, I'm going to take a quick stroll in the garden before I meet you in the great hall."

"I hope I shall have no regrets about this," the king said.

"What is there to regret? She is a lovely girl. You'll see."

And with that, the queen left, not wanting to discuss it any further. She gathered her furs and made her way to the garden, looking to speak to the gardener to finalize matters with him.

As she walked, she recalled the conversation with the king. Of course, she didn't *need* to make Violet princess. It was necessary only to keep the girl long enough for her to turn eleven years of age and to demonstrate how to interact with the birds. The spell for beauty was still *the* most important matter to the queen.

But Bogdana had noticed something yesterday as she gathered clues about the girl: her supposed interactions with the birds, the playfulness she exhibited in the garden, and her simple yet honest artwork. The girl had a tremendous love of life, despite the miserable life that it was, like no one the queen had met before. And then to be beautiful, too? She was like a rare gem, and the queen simply had to have her. And maybe, just maybe, if love came so easily to the girl, perhaps someday she would find room in her heart to love the queen, too.

Just the simple thought made the queen happy.

A moment later, she came upon George pruning some bushes.

"There you are," the queen said. "I've been looking for you."

He bowed. "Your Majesty."

"I will not ask about your night in the dungeon for I'm sure you would rather not relive it. I've come to speak to you about the secret garden."

"What about it?"

"I want it destroyed. Move what plants you can and get rid of the rest. When the birds return, they mustn't go there. They shall live in my garden instead."

"Surely there's another way," George said. "That garden is like a home to Violet. It will crush her if it's destroyed."

The queen waved a dismissive hand. "The child will be fine. She has so much more to make her happy now. A silly little garden is nothing compared to all she will be given in the coming days."

"But I fear, Your Highness, there are risks. What if the birds fly elsewhere? Away from the castle?"

"But the girl is *here*," the queen said. "From what I've been told, I believe they will come to see her. So there will be no more discussion. My request shall be granted. By the time the girl is crowned princess, the secret garden shall be no more. Understood?"

"Understood."

"Good. Carry on."

George bowed again. "Yes, Your Majesty. As you wish."

The queen smiled with pleasure at three of her favorite words before returning to the castle.

23

*B*ogdana stood in Violet's bedchamber, her mouth agape.

"What is it?" Violet asked, smoothing the skirt of the emerald gown she wore. "Is something wrong? Did I choose the wrong dress for the occasion?"

The queen shook her head and blinked her eyes, as if she was trying to see straight. "No, no, nothing is wrong. Quite the contrary. Your hair braided and the lovely dress...why, you are simply stunning."

Violet felt her shoulders relax. "Oh, good. I was worried for a moment."

"Let's make our way to the great hall, shall we?"

"Yes," Violet said, and she followed the queen through the maze of hallways and stairways until they came to the large room where people sat and ate. They approached the high table, and in the center, next to the king, were two empty chairs. As the king rose to greet them, so did everyone else.

"Violet," he said, extending his hand.

"King Louis," she replied, taking the king's hand and kissing it as she curtsied, the way her mother had taught her. At the time, Violet had laughed because it seemed so unlikely she would ever need to know how to greet the king.

Once Violet sat down, servants brought dish after dish of food. So much glorious food! She started to ask the queen what the various dishes were, but as the queen stuffed herself with a large chunk of meat, the juices seeping into a flat piece of bread held beneath it, she decided against it. Violet simply did as the queen did and began eating.

Violet had never tasted such good food, and she

began to wonder if she might actually come to enjoy being a princess. In fact, she probably wouldn't have to choke down another boiled egg as long as she lived. While Violet ate, she sensed people's eyes on her. It made her nervous. Would they be happy when they heard the plans to crown her princess? Or would they be angry, for surely it would mean extra work for everyone one way or another.

While Violet munched on her fourth piece of boiled potato seasoned with parsley and onion, the king stood and clapped his hands quickly three times.

"You may have noticed," he began, "we have a new face at our table this fine day. Because of a tragic accident, we have taken custody of this child named Violet. To officially welcome her into the family, we shall have a royal ball six weeks from now, on the spring equinox. On that day, we will crown her Princess Violet. Let the preparations begin!"

The room erupted with applause. Violet's cheeks grew warm, for she wasn't used to all this attention.

She turned and looked at the queen, who now smiled as if the room were filled with colorful humming-birds. It seemed so strange that the queen could be so happy about a girl she hardly knew.

As the applause died down, the king took his seat.

"You may go now, Violet," the queen said. "It is not proper for a child to linger at the table as we do. Return to your room and rest, for your lessons will begin tomorrow, and as you are to discover, they shall be quite rigorous."

Violet stood and gave a small curtsy before she stepped down and away from the tables. As she walked back the way they had come, she realized she didn't want to return to her room and rest. She'd been in that room long enough. Wasn't there something else she could do? Somewhere else to explore?

As she turned a corner, she almost ran into a short, skinny boy about her age, wearing a dirty tunic and smelling of onions.

"Pardon me, miss," he said. "I thought everyone was still eating."

"Who are you?" Violet asked.

"The name's Harry," he said. "I work in the kitchen."

"Oh!" Violet's eyes lit up. "The kitchen. I've never seen a kitchen before. Will you show me?"

"And who are you?" Harry asked.

"I'm Violet," she replied. "I've come to live here and will be crowned princess soon."

His eyes narrowed. "Wait a minute. Are you pulling my leg? Violet? Ain't that the name of the girl in the tower?"

Violet looked around, hoping no one had heard him say that. "Yes, that's me. But no one knows I was locked in the tower. We must keep it a secret. How did you know, anyway?"

"Maggie let your name slip one time, when she came to the kitchen to gather your food. Don't worry. I'm the only one who heard it."

"I'm pleased to meet you, Harry, and thank you for

the food, if you helped at all. Will you show me the kitchen? Please?"

Harry shrugged. "Why not? Follow me."

They made their way through a long corridor, then down a flight of stairs, into a room with copper pots and stone ovens covering one wall. On another wall, there was a big open pit with a large fire burning to heat not only a huge black cauldron but also a large chunk of meat, which two boys turned on a long pole. In the middle of the room were rows of tables where three young men stood chopping vegetables and kneading dough. Violet thought the room smelled delicious.

"This is it," Harry said.

"Who's she?" one of the young men said.

"Violet," Harry replied. "She'll be crowned princess one day." Harry looked around. "Where's Cook?"

"A delivery wagon carrying goods for the castle lost a wheel," another young man replied. "He and Elmer went down the road to help."

"Good. Come on. I can show you the pantry real quick."

Harry led Violet outside, around a corner, through a door, and down a dark set of stairs. The earthy smell as they descended reminded Violet of the garden after a hard rain, although it had more of a stench about it.

When they reached the final step, Violet looked around the dark room, lit only by a burning oil lamp set on the table. Barrels lined the walls in the very back, while the nearby walls were covered with strings of onions, mushrooms, and other vegetables hung to dry.

"What are those for?" Violet asked, pointing to a couple of large hooks that hung from the ceiling.

"That's where we put the chickens in order to pluck them."

Violet shuddered at the thought.

"This is where food and drink is stored," Harry explained. "Elmer, the pantler, works down here. Since he's busy at the moment, I thought you might like to see—"

Before Harry could finish, Violet felt something rubbing against her leg. She let out a high-pitched scream and grabbed on to Harry's arm, hopping from foot to foot.

Harry laughed. "The cats."

"Cats?" Violet asked, standing still. "There are cats down here?"

"Aye. There is. To catch the rats and mice."

"Oh dear. The queen told me about rats. They sound like awful creatures. Cats are nicer, then? I've never seen any animals, unless you count the birds in the garden."

"A couple of the cats are skittish, but this one here"—he bent down and scooped it into his arms—"he's friendly. I call him Lucky. 'Cause we're lucky to have such a fine mouse catcher. Do you want to pet him?"

Violet watched for a moment and decided he seemed gentle enough. When she touched his fur, she smiled, for she'd never felt anything quite like it.

Harry seemed to be studying the girl. Violet wondered if he thought it strange to meet someone who knew so little of the world. She was about to ask him about it when he said, "Can I tell you a secret?"

"Of course," Violet said.

"I was looking for the queen yesterday 'cause Cook sent me to ask her something about the meal. When I went to her bedchamber, I heard her in there with Maggie. It sounded like she cast…" He paused, as if he was unsure whether he should say it.

"What? Go on. What did it sound like?"

"It sounded like she cast a spell on the poor woman."

"Whatever do you mean?"

"What I mean is, I think the queen is actually a witch. Do you know what a witch is?"

"Someone who uses magic?" Violet asked.

Before Harry could respond, they heard a noise

coming from outside. Harry dropped the cat and took Violet's hand. "Come on. Time to go. Won't be good for either of us if Cook finds you down here."

"Wait. Where are we going?" Violet asked as he grabbed the oil lantern and pulled her deep into the pantry.

"There's a secret passageway," he told her. "The castle is full of them. This one isn't very long and takes you right outside the kitchen. You can find your way from there. I'll hold the lamp while you go on through, aye? There's another one I can show you someday, if you'd like. It's the best one of 'em all."

Violet smiled at the thought of secret passageways hidden throughout the castle. "Oh, I'd love to see it," she said as he pushed hard on a spot in the wall, causing it to move so it revealed a slight opening. "And you have to tell me more about the queen and Maggie. I want to know more of your suspicions."

"Aye, but remember, it's our secret!"

"I know. I hope to see you again soon."

He hurried her along. As Violet walked through the dark and narrow passageway, she thought about how she couldn't wait to see Harry again.

"A friend," she whispered, smiling. "I think I've found a friend."

24

The first night of her freedom, Nuri didn't make it to the nearest village before she needed to rest for the night. With little physical activity over the past several years, she walked slowly and became tired quickly.

The area surrounding the castle had acres and acres of farmland, and every now and then, she would pass a farmhouse. Fortunately, she spotted an empty chicken coop behind a vacant house. In the event the residents might return, she decided the coop would make a fine place to bed down. She ate the bread and jerky as the sun set, and thought of her daughter falling asleep on a soft bed with a warm fire aglow in the room. At long last, Violet would have all the things she so richly deserved.

She knew, however, that Violet would feel sad and somewhat alone without her mother, and she wished on the stars in the sky that Violet wasn't missing her too deeply. Exhausted after all that had happened, Nuri lay down on the dirt floor in the coop and slept the whole night through.

She awoke to a light pitter-patter on the roof the next morning. Instinctively, Nuri reached over for Violet, to tell her to listen for the rain. But when she opened her eyes, a sea of sadness washed over her, and she lay there for a while until it passed.

When she stepped outside and into the mist, she noticed that with the rain had come warmer temperatures. It wasn't long before she returned to the road that led to the village, baskets in hand. After the light rain shower passed, the sun peeked through the clouds. Nuri nibbled on some bread, thankful Maggie had provided enough to last her for a while.

As she got closer to town, people joined her on the road, talking and laughing among themselves. She was in luck—it was market day. As she listened in on the conversations, she became aware of how much she had missed being around others. And how good it felt to move. Her legs were sore from the walking she'd done the previous day, but she didn't mind. To be outside, in air that smelled fresh and clean, surrounded by others, was a dream come true. She couldn't deny that it gave her a renewed sense of hope.

In the market square, crowds of people bustled about, wandering from table to table, where food and household items could be purchased. There weren't any performers in the square yet. This was fortunate for Nuri, although she still wasn't sure she could manage on her own. She'd always had her family with her, not only for the performing part, but also for the collection of the coins.

Nuri began to turn away, thinking maybe this had been a bad idea. And then she saw a girl with beautiful black hair and bright blue eyes walk by her. If Violet were here, she would tell her mother to not be afraid. That she must perform and make money so she could set out and find her Marko.

After taking a deep breath, Nuri grabbed her tambourine and sang. At first, she performed softly, passing the tambourine back and forth between her hands, getting used to the rhythm and feel of the instrument.

As her playing intensified, so did her voice, and soon she had captured the interest of a number of market-goers.

When she finished the first song, the crowd applauded. She bowed and very subtly pointed to the basket. A man walked up and dropped a coin into it.

Nuri thanked him, and soon a couple more did the same.

Nuri continued singing and collecting coins for the next few hours, until her throat became so dry she had to stop. She looked around, searching for the old man with the white beard and mustache Maggie and George had told her about. It took a while, but she eventually found him.

She made her way to him, eyeing the delicious vegetables he had for sale. "Hello, Richard," she said. "My name is Nuri. I am a friend of George and Maggie's. They said to look for you here. My daughter is still there, and they'll be sending messages through you to let me know how she is doing."

He nodded as he offered her a drink from his goatskin bag. "Of course. They are fine people, and any friend of theirs is a friend of mine. But I'm not quite sure I understand. Why did your daughter stay on at the castle if you are no longer there?"

Nuri finished drinking, wiped her chin, and handed

Richard his bag. Then she proceeded to tell him the story of being trapped in the tower and the queen's sudden desire to take Violet as her own child.

"I am sorry for your troubles," he said. "And I'm pleased to help you any way I can. I must say, you have a lovely singing voice. But 'tis not safe to travel alone. Where's the rest of your family, lass? Do you know?"

"Not sure, I'm 'fraid. That's why I'm performing. I must earn enough so that I can go in search of them. You haven't seen any wandering minstrels recently, have you?"

He shook his head. "Can't say I have. They usually travel to warmer weather this time of year. Surely you remember that."

"Aye. I do believe you're right. I wish I could go looking for them now. But I'll have to stay and work for a time."

He handed her an onion and a handful of beans. "Best o' luck to you. I'll be sure to let you know if any messages come your way."

"Thanks to you, Richard. I'm glad to have a friendly face here, that's for sure."

They said good-bye, and Nuri wandered around the marketplace, munching on the onion like an apple, admiring the shoes, woven cloths, and pottery being sold.

In the far corner of the square, she found an old woman selling colorful scarves. One of the scarves was a lovely purple color, and as she fingered the fabric, Nuri got a lump in her throat, thinking of her daughter and her pretty eyes. Oh, how she wanted to purchase the scarf. But the price was high, and there was no money to spare on frivolous items.

When the people of the market began to pack up, Nuri headed back to the chicken coop. In the distance, the sun tiptoed quietly behind the hills, signaling the end of another day.

While she was in the tower, the love of her daughter, along with the hope of seeing her husband again, had sustained her day in and day out. Now all she had left was hope.

She closed her eyes and felt the cool breeze on her cheek, like a kiss from Mother Nature, reassuring her everything would be fine. And she knew all she could do was believe in that promise.

25

*T*he minstrels and the birds had begun their journey back toward the castle. The birds had become accustomed to the rhythm of the minstrels' days and nights, and they felt comfortable with them.

One day, as the group of musicians walked along, singing and laughing, one of them pointed up in the air. The birds, curious as to what the minstrels saw, looked up, higher than they ever flew.

And there, with wings spread long and full, reaching to the far sides of the sky, was a hawk.

To humans, hawks are beautiful birds in flight.

To hummingbirds, hawks are enemies.

The two small birds watched as the hawk dove down, aiming straight for them.

The birds had to be quick and find a place to hide.

Faster and faster the hawk came, closer and closer. If given the chance, it could grab one of the humming-birds with its talons midair, and off it'd go.

Fortunately, the two birds spotted a row of old blackberry brambles and headed there. Although the leaves and berries hadn't begun to grow back yet, the twisted brambles would provide a safe place to hide from the hawk.

The hummingbirds flew quickly, their wings buzz-ing as they went. The minstrels watched, their mouths open, as the hawk dove through the air, obviously chasing something.

Peace and Pax made it to the brambles just as the hawk tried to grab Peace. The hawk stuck around a moment, waiting to see if the small birds would re-appear. But they stayed safely put. And so the hawk moved on, searching for new prey.

As it flew back into the sky, the minstrels waved good-bye.

The hummingbirds felt thankful for the minstrels, who not only sang lovely songs, but also spotted scary things in the sky. Now more than ever, the birds wanted to introduce the girl in the tower to these kind and happy people.

26

The days following Violet's arrival in the castle were a whirlwind of activity. She was given daily lessons on social graces: how to walk like a lady, how to sit properly, how to use a needle and thread, how to write correspondence, how to dance, and, yes, how to play the harp. The harp lessons, which Maggie had arranged herself with one of the castle's employed minstrels, were by far Violet's favorite.

Various ladies-in-waiting, sent to the castle by their relatives to receive an education, became Violet's teachers on all matters. She was told again and again by every one of the ladies that six weeks was not nearly enough time to teach her everything she should know.

They simply hoped she would learn enough to avoid making a fool of herself the night of the ball.

After three weeks of nearly nonstop lessons, Violet awoke, rolled over, and heaved a great sigh.

"Now, now," Maggie said, rushing around, collecting the child's clothing. "We'll have none of that. Lady Sarah is expecting you in the ballroom for another dance lesson this morning."

"Maggie, must I go today? Can't I visit my garden instead and see if there is any sign of the birds? I do miss them so."

"'Tis still too cold, lass. You must wait a bit longer, for spring will be here soon." She paused. "While we're talking about the birds, there's something I must tell you."

Violet sat up, her eyes wide. "What? What is it, Maggie? Please, let it not be bad news."

"'Fraid it is. The queen has ordered George to destroy your little garden behind the tower. She wants the birds to live in the main garden when they return."

"Oh no," Violet said, her eyes filling with tears as she climbed out of bed. "But I love that garden. And it's the birds' home. They love it there as much as I do."

"I know," Maggie said as she pulled Violet's nightclothes off her. "I'm sorry to be the one to tell you."

"Has he started the work yet?" Violet asked, wrapping her arms around herself as Maggie gathered up a lovely dress the color of sunshine.

"Hold your arms up," Maggie said. Violet did as she was told, and Maggie slipped the dress over her head. "No, he hasn't started on it yet. But soon."

Violet fingered the elegant fabric and wondered how much such a thing cost. Every day she'd worn something new. At first, it was exciting. Now it seemed almost strange. Why did a simple young girl need so many clothes?

"Perhaps I should try speaking to the queen about it. If she truly cares about me, she'll listen to what I have to say," Violet said. "I'm not just a doll she can dress up and show off. I have feelings, too. She needs to know that."

She bit her lip as her mother flittered into her thoughts. Her mother had always listened to what Violet had to say, caring about her feelings more than her own. She started to say something about how much she missed her but stopped herself. She was already feeling blue, and it would do no good to make it worse.

Maggie took the girl's chin and lifted it up so Violet's eyes met hers. "I wouldn't recommend going to battle with the queen. Trust me, she always wins. Her mind is made up, love, and that's that. But I do believe the birds will be just fine, for they shall still have you, eh?"

"I suppose," Violet said with a sigh. "It won't be the same, though."

"Come along," Maggie said. "Let's finish getting you ready, and then you can have some tea and a freshly baked tart."

A short while later, Violet went down the stairs

toward the ballroom. Maggie had other duties to attend to, so she'd left the child to make her way on her own. Violet took her time, counting to ten each time she landed on a step, wanting to delay another day of lessons as long as she possibly could.

"Pssst," she heard from behind her. "Violet. Come here."

She turned around to find Harry standing there, wearing a dirty tunic. A grin spread across her face. *Finally!* She'd been wondering when she would see him again.

She dashed to where he stood. He took her hand, put his finger to his lips telling her to be quiet, and led her around the corner. And then, before she knew what was happening, he pushed the wall in and they ducked into a small room. The wall, or door, or whatever it was, clicked shut behind them. A small candle sat on a shelf built into the wall on the far corner, and Violet was thankful for the light.

"Another passageway!" she exclaimed, scanning the tiny room with her eyes. In front of them, a set of stairs extended down into a hole of darkness.

"Aye. 'Tis something else, eh?"

"What are the secret passageways for?" Violet asked.

"In case of an unexpected invasion. With this particular one, the king and queen have an easy—but discreet—way to escape."

"Where does it lead?"

"Outside the castle. It twists and turns and takes you all the way down near the pantry. 'Tis how I found it. One day, I headed outside from the kitchen, to fetch some mushrooms for the cook. I leaned up against the wall to catch my breath, and when I did, the wall moved. I pushed on it a few times, and the wall opened up. This was the first of the passageways I found. Since then, I've discovered others, like the one I showed you the last time we met. But I wanted to show you this one especially, so I brought a candle along before I went to look for you."

"I'm so happy to see you again. Thank you for finding me."

"The queen is keeping you busy, eh?"

Violet sighed. "'Tis true. In fact, I mustn't stay long. But I want to learn more of your suspicions about the queen."

"Like I told you, I believe her to be a witch. By that I mean someone with magical powers. She cast a spell on Maggie that day—I'm sure of it. After the queen insisted Maggie drink from a goblet, she said some strange lines about the sun and the moon and seeking the truth. A moment later, she asked Maggie to tell her about the hummingbirds."

Violet gasped. "Did you hear Maggie's response?"

Shadows loomed on the wall behind the boy. He leaned in slightly, and Violet noticed then that his nose was quite crooked. She stared at his nose while he told her what he'd heard. "Aye. She said, 'The hummingbirds live in a secret garden.' That's all I know, for someone was coming down the hallway, and I didn't want to get caught listening."

"A witch with magical powers," Violet whispered, her eyes big and round. "Could it truly be so?"

"I believe it is."

"Wait. Did you say you heard this exchange the day before you met me in the castle?"

"Aye."

A hand flew to Violet's mouth. "That must be how the queen found me! Maggie told her of the secret garden, through no fault of her own, and the queen went to see it for herself. Now it all makes sense."

"If she is a witch, and I certainly think she is, I fear for your safety, Violet. What if she wants you for some strange spell?"

"Or the birds," Violet said, remembering how the queen had spoken about them with such longing. "She is completely infatuated with the birds." She grabbed Harry's arms. "When the hummingbirds return, she wants me to get them to trust her as they trust me. She is destroying the secret garden so they will live in her garden instead. What shall we do? I cannot let anything happen to the sweet birds."

"Perhaps we should plan for your escape," he replied.

"In order to keep you and the birds safe from potential harm."

"But if I were caught, surely she would throw me in the dungeon," Violet said, her legs trembling at the thought.

"I wish we knew what she is up to," Harry said.

"I'm sorry. I must go, for I am expected in the ballroom," Violet said. "Thank you for finding me and showing me this passageway."

"I'm pleased to have done so," he replied. "It might come in handy for you someday, as a hiding place, perhaps. Or a way to escape, if the opportunity arises. You never know."

Violet nodded and then Harry pushed on the wall ever so slightly, just enough to scan the hallway. "All is clear," he said. He grabbed the candle and pointed in the opposite direction, toward the stairs. "I'm going to head out this way. You run along to your lessons. I may see if I can snoop around the queen's bedchamber. Perhaps I can find clues about her plans."

"Do be careful, Harry. I would hate for anything to happen to you on my account."

He pushed the door all the way, and Violet stepped outside. "Please don't worry about me," he told her. "Look after yourself, for I shall be fine."

"I hope so," Violet whispered to herself as she rushed back to the staircase.

A little later, when she arrived in the ballroom, Lady Sarah said, "You are late. We talked about the importance of being on time, did we not?"

Violet bowed her head. "I beg your pardon. It shall not happen again."

"Fine. Let us begin, then. Arms up, back straight, smile, please. And one and two and three…"

As Violet performed the steps Lady Sarah taught her, she tried to forget about Harry's suspicions of the queen. But of course, it was all she could think about.

27

For two weeks, Harry looked for an opportunity to sneak into the queen's bedchamber to search for clues as to whether his fears about her were true, and if she had anything sinister planned for Violet or the hummingbirds. But for some reason, Cook seemed to be keeping an extra-close eye on him.

"Sweet Josephine, what's wrong with you lately, boy?" he'd asked Harry one day as he chopped onions. "You're slower than a mule after plowin' day. Got something on your mind?"

"No, sir," Harry had replied.

"Then for pity's sake, stop daydreaming and chop faster!"

Harry thought he saw doubt in the cook's eyes. Had he seen Harry sneaking off to show Violet the passageway? He'd tried to be very careful, but he had an uneasy feeling about it. As difficult as it was, with big questions looming, Harry didn't wander far.

Finally, Harry decided he could wait no more. He knew that with the royal ball right around the corner, Violet must be filled with worry. He simply had to find out what, if anything, the queen had planned.

While some of the longtime servants had been given hovels behind the castle to live in, Harry and the rest of the kitchen staff, along with the guards and stable boys, slept in the great hall. This was the castle way, after all. During the day, the large, multipurpose room was used to feed everyone. At night, they pushed the tables and chairs away and used the space for sleeping. The staff fell to the floor, exhausted after a long day's work, covering themselves with a coat or blanket.

One night, Harry lay there long after everyone fell

asleep, watching the moon through the window until it was high in the sky. Then, ever so quietly, he made his way to the queen's chamber. The king's bedchamber was across the hall, so fortunately, he would only have to concern himself with not disturbing the queen.

When Harry reached his destination, he could hear her snores from the other side of the wall. This was a good sign, he thought. Slowly and carefully, he opened the door. When it made a slight creak, he stopped, held his breath, and waited. But the queen didn't move.

Once he was inside, the glow from the fire provided him with enough light to be able to see around the chamber, just as he had expected. But as he looked around, he realized perhaps this hadn't been such a wise idea after all. He didn't even know what he might be searching for. If the queen had plans for the young girl or the birds, what might tell him so? Notes to herself? Strange objects set aside, ready to be made into a spell? He saw none of this in the room.

And then his eyes landed on a large book opened on a table near the hearth. As he tiptoed toward it, the queen let out a loud snort and rolled over. Harry crouched, afraid she might open her eyes briefly as she stirred. There, close to the ground and with a racing heart, he waited until her snores were slow and rhythmic once again.

On his hands and knees, he crawled across the floor, quiet as a cat. When he reached the table, he stood and took in the book, which appeared to be quite old. It was open to a page that said "The Spell for Beauty."

While most boys working in the castle didn't know how to read, Harry did because of the kindness of the pantler, Elmer. Harry had begged Elmer to teach him until he gave in. Harry was an orphan who had been fortunate enough to get a job working at the castle instead of begging on the streets or, worse, being forced to labor in a workhouse, where conditions, rumor had it, were dismal.

Now, looking at the book, Harry was thankful he hadn't given up on his quest for learning.

The spell for beauty is a powerful one, Harry read to himself. *It requires two special and rare ingredients that come from creatures of great beauty.*

The first is a long hair the color of darkness plucked from

the head of a girl with lavender eyes who has lived at least eleven years but no more than twelve. The second is a single feather from a living hummingbird, the smallest and most beautiful of all birds.

Harry had found his answer, and he was filled with relief that no harm would have to come to Violet or the birds. However, he knew he must relay the information to his friend as soon as possible.

Very quickly, he scanned the page to make sure there was nothing else of importance, but found the rest of the ingredients to be quite common and the incantation to be long and tedious.

As Harry turned to leave, the queen moaned and stirred once again. This time, Harry dropped to the ground and lay as flat as he could on the floor underneath the table.

He watched as the queen sat straight up and called out, "Is someone there?"

The boy held his breath and kept as still as a dead

mouse, hoping the shadows in the room were such that she wouldn't spot him.

A minute felt like an hour, but eventually the queen settled back into her bed. Harry waited until her snores started up again, and then he snuck out of her room and into the safety of the hallway.

28

Most of the market-goers and merchants were kind to Nuri. Word spread of her desire to find her husband, and so, when she played twice a week at the marketplace, they paid her well and offered up food and drink to assist her. She was grateful for their generosity and believed that by spring she would have enough to go in search of him.

Every market day, she checked with Richard to see if he had received a message from the castle. And every time, he shook his head and said, "I'm truly sorry, Nuri. But don't give up hope."

Hope. She clung to it at night, along with her favorite of the wooden figurines, the one of the girl with a bird in her hand. And during the day, when she wasn't performing, she went house to house seeking odd jobs and met mothers and daughters who caused her to cling to it harder still.

One morning, Nuri entered the market square walking as if she carried a bag of bricks on her back. For hope, at times, is fleeting, like a tiny hummingbird—there one moment, gone the next. That morning, she wondered how she could possibly live another day without knowing that her daughter was all right. What if the queen hadn't kept her promises? What if she'd put the poor girl to work rather than treating her as she deserved to be treated, like a true princess?

Numerous scenarios, none of them good, filled Nuri's head, and she didn't know how she could muster the enthusiasm to perform in the square another day. She reached her usual spot, picked up her tambourine, and closed her eyes for a moment. The memory was so clear, it was as if it had happened yes-terday.

What shall you draw this time?

A picture of you, Papa, and me. Smiling because we are so thankful to be free.

Nuri knew, no matter how sad she might be, it was up to her to bring her family together. With a new resolve, she was about to begin to play when she felt a tap on her shoulder. She turned to find Richard standing there with a large grin on his face.

"I have news," he told her, "of your dear daughter."

"Oh, thank heavens," Nuri exclaimed. "What have you heard?"

He looked around at the people who had begun to gather, and motioned for her to follow him back to his vegetable stand.

"Richard, I cannot wait a second longer," Nuri said when they reached his spot. "Please, tell me."

He leaned in and whispered, his brown eyes shiny

like rocks in a river, "She is getting along splendidly. She adores her large bed in her private bedchamber, where she sleeps warm and comfortably. She's eating well, and Maggie says you'd be amazed how healthy the young girl looks."

Nuri smiled as she gripped Richard's sleeve. "Who sent the message? Did Maggie come herself, and I somehow missed her?"

"It wasn't Maggie. A boy named Harry came along with the cook to buy goods at the market, and Maggie asked him to bring the message. She felt he could be trusted not to breathe a word of it to the queen."

"Oh, bless you, Harry," Nuri whispered, looking up at the sky before returning her eyes to the man. "Did he say anything else?"

"Aye!" he said, his eyes wide. "I have yet to tell you the best part. She is learning many social graces in preparation for the royal ball they are holding in her honor on the eve of the spring equinox. It is then Violet will be crowned princess."

Nuri's hand flew to her mouth as her other hand squeezed Richard's arm to steady herself. "A royal ball? For Violet?"

"Maggie said she is doing remarkably well with her lessons. She is a wonderful student, and if you were there, you would be very proud of her."

Nuri shook her head in disbelief. "Oh my word. I *am* proud of her."

" 'Tis a shame you can't be there to see your daughter at the ball."

"I know," Nuri said softly, her face drooping slightly. "I suppose I will just have to imagine it all." She looked Richard in the eye. "Thank you. A million times, thank you."

Nuri turned to leave, but Richard said, "Wait. There is one more thing Harry wanted you to know. 'Tis not a message from Maggie, but from the boy himself."

Richard motioned for her to come closer, and he whispered in her ear, "There is a secret passageway inside the castle that leads to the outside. Harry made sure to show your daughter, in the event she decides she wants to try to escape the evil queen's clutches."

This latest piece of news made Nuri pause. Could Violet really attempt an escape? Given her new circumstances, would she even want to?

"Are you all right?" Richard asked. "Did I do more harm than good in sharing that with you?"

Nuri thought of the girl she'd known in the tower. The girl who wasn't afraid to sneak down to the garden every day to see her beloved birds. The girl who spoke of freedom and longed to meet her papa. And the girl who claimed that if she could survive living in a tower for ten years, she could do anything. If an opportunity arose for Violet to escape, of course she would take it. And she needed to know where to go if she did.

"I am glad you told me," Nuri assured her new friend.

"Shall I try to get a message to your daughter the next time I see the kitchen boy?" Richard asked.

"Tell him to let Violet know I am here. That if she ever wants to try to find me, I'm here in the market square on Wednesdays and Saturdays." Nuri paused. "And please tell her how much I love her."

Richard smiled. "Consider it done."

29

*T*he bed filled with feathers was indeed a thing of delight to lie on. And yet, Violet's nights weren't exactly restful. She continued to dream of her mother and would often wake up reaching for her.

One morning, she woke early, and try as she might, she could not fall back to sleep. It was so early Maggie had not yet come to assist her with dressing. Violet crawled out of the big bed and climbed onto the window seat.

She strummed the harp for a while, finding comfort in its music. The minstrel had called her a natural. He'd told her it would please the king and queen greatly if Violet were able to play a song the night of

the ball. So she practiced a particular piece over and over again.

Soon she grew tired of playing and turned to look out the window at the garden. She longed to see her flying friends.

When the door opened a few minutes later, she thought it would be Maggie. She turned to say good morning and was surprised to find Harry standing there instead.

"I could hear your harp from down the hall," Harry said, his face red as he looked at the floor, "so I knew you were awake."

"Please, turn around," Violet said. "I am in my night-clothes and not properly dressed."

Harry did as she asked. "My sincere apologies. Please know I wouldn't have come if it weren't impor-tant. I have news to tell you. And it's difficult to find you alone these days."

"What is it, Harry? What do you wish to tell me?"

He quickly told her of the book he'd found in the queen's chamber and the ingredients the beauty spell required.

Violet listened carefully, and as she did, anger bubbled up inside her and she could feel her cheeks getting warm. All the misery, all the years spent without her papa, all the heartache both she and her mother had endured, and for what?

Because the queen wanted one thing and one thing only—to be beautiful.

"Tell me what the spell said," Violet said. "Exactly. Word for word, if you are able."

She listened intently as Harry told her the words he'd apparently taken to memory.

"The spell of beauty is a powerful one. It requires two special and rare ingredients that come from creatures of great beauty. The first is a long hair the color of darkness plucked from the head of a girl with lavender eyes who has lived at least eleven years but no more than twelve. The second is a single feather from a living hummingbird, the smallest and most beautiful of all birds."

Of course, Violet had always wondered why the queen had done it. Why she'd imprisoned the two of them. She and her mother had talked about it over the years. Nothing had made much sense, except perhaps that it had been a harsh punishment for trespassing.

But now Violet knew the awful, ugly truth.

She didn't speak for quite a long while. "Are you all right?" Harry asked. "At least you're not in danger, eh?"

"That is true," Violet said. "Still, to have been trapped for so long all because of a wish as frivolous as beauty? Makes my blood boil."

"Before I return to the kitchen, I have one more thing to tell you," Harry said. "It is about your mother. She sends her love and wants you to know she is in the market square on Wednesdays and Saturdays, performing."

This was all Violet needed to hear. She knew what she must do now. "Harry?"

"Aye?" he replied, his back still to her.

"Am I correct in assuming the day of the ball will be quite busy?" Violet asked.

"Busy indeed," Harry replied.

"Then I shall need your help," Violet whispered, "for it seems to me the perfect day to attempt an escape." With a sly smile, she added, "Some assistance with a special *surprise* for the queen between now and then would be appreciated as well."

30

*T*he ball was only a few days away, and the queen could hardly contain her excitement. The preparations were coming along splendidly, and Violet was doing well with her lessons. Soon a princess would be crowned, the birds would return to her garden, and Bogdana's wishes would come true.

With all the joyful anticipation, she practically floated through the castle as she made her way to the great hall for the midday meal. But when she arrived at her table, she let out a scream and almost fainted from the ghastly sight that awaited her there.

"What have you done?" she shrieked.

Violet looked at her with innocent eyes. "Are you speaking to me?"

"Who else would I be speaking to? Your hair, child. It's . . . gone!"

Violet patted her head, where only slight fuzz, like that of a peach, remained. "Indeed it is."

The queen shook her head in disbelief. "But why?" She looked around. "And who is responsible for this travesty? Speak now, or you will face even greater punishment than a night in the dungeon."

"Please," the king said, "Bogdana, you must calm down. 'Twas a bad case of lice, the child told me. She had no choice but to shear it off. She's young and healthy, and of course it will grow back. Now, sit down so we may eat."

"I shall not sit down," the queen yelled. "Perhaps you do not understand how dire this situation is. Surely we must postpone the ball, for we cannot crown a princess looking like... *that!*"

Violet rose to her feet and faced the queen. "I have been working very hard to prepare for the ball, Your Majesty. As I understand it, the refreshments have been purchased, the announcements have been made, and many people are traveling from near and far for the occasion. And you wish to cancel it because of something as frivolous as my hair?"

"It is not frivolous," the queen bellowed. "You look hideous, and I will not have you make a fool of me."

"Certainly beauty is not a royal requirement, is it, Your Majesty?" Violet asked. "I have always believed it's what's on the inside that counts. After all, I would rather have a heart of gold than a face that is envied, wouldn't you agree?"

As Violet spoke of beauty and a face to be envied, the queen suddenly realized the ball was the least of her worries. Without a single hair on the girl's head, it would be impossible to cast the spell for beauty until her hair grew out. Bogdana would have to wait many months, perhaps even a year, for a strand that was long enough.

The queen ignored Violet's inquiry and instead shouted, "Maggie?"

"Yes, Your Majesty?" Maggie replied as she rose from her seat.

The queen glared at her. "When we are finished with our meal, I shall have a word with you. Privately.

For I hold you partially responsible for this most un-fortunate circumstance."

Maggie curtsied. "As you wish, my queen."

With nothing left to say, Bogdana sank into her seat, consumed with disappointment.

Violet turned to the king. "Pray tell, am I correct?" she asked him. "Surely beauty, which we have little con-trol over, is not a royal requirement."

"You are correct," he replied. "There are far more important qualities than beauty. And from what I've seen, Violet, you possess many great characteristics that will make you a fine princess."

The king turned to address everyone seated in the great hall. "The royal ball will go on as scheduled, and very soon, we shall have a princess among us!"

The crowd cheered as the queen sulked. If only the ancient spell book could help her, but she knew it was useless, as there hadn't been anything written about speeding up hair growth. She would simply have to be patient and wait for Violet's hair to grow out.

Bogdana sighed in frustration. Hadn't she been patient long enough? She glared at Violet, and thought the young girl seemed almost happy about this latest development. And the king seemed completely taken by her.

In fact, as the queen scanned the faces in the great hall, all eyes were on Violet. *Everyone* was taken by the girl. The queen's frustration and disappointment quickly turned to fury.

They were supposed to be a team, the child and the queen. They were to be admired together. Envied together. *Beautiful* together.

Well, how dare Violet get in the way of the queen's well-laid plans?

Perhaps the king could insist the ball go on as scheduled. But if Violet were to disappear without a trace the day of the ball, the queen thought as she schemed, what could he possibly do about that?

For hair could grow out in the dungeon just as well as it could grow out in the castle.

31

*P*eace and Pax followed the minstrels as they made their way toward the castle. Every day, the temperature grew warmer, and their little hearts grew ever more hopeful that soon the girl whom they'd come to love in the garden would be reunited with her father and finally set free.

As they traveled along, the two hummingbirds spread word to all their winged friends of the reunion soon to take place. The minstrels, preoccupied with trying to help Marko regain his memory, didn't notice the growing number of butterflies, bees, and hummingbirds flying in the fields around them.

Finally, one lovely morning, when it felt as if winter

might be gone for good, the two hummingbirds recognized the scenery and knew the castle was nearby. The birds watched as the minstrels began dancing for joy. In fact, they danced and sang all the way up to the castle.

"Halt," exclaimed a young man as he extended his shiny lance. "What business do you have at the castle this day?"

"We are here to seek answers," said one of the minstrels. "We are here to find a woman and a young child whom we believe were taken from us."

"I cannot let you enter," the guard said.

"Please," an older man said, "let a couple of us pass through. You do not need to tell anyone. We shall gladly pay you for your troubles." He extended a bag bulging at the seams with coins.

But the young man standing guard at the gate shook his head. "I have taken an oath, and I must protect the king and queen at all costs. Now, be on your way, for we are expecting many important people for a royal ball this evening."

As the minstrels continued in their efforts to convince the guard to let them through, Peace and Pax, along with all of their friends who had joined them on the journey to the castle, made their way to the garden.

Perhaps wandering minstrels weren't welcome beyond the gate, but birds, bees, and butterflies certainly were.

32

On the day of the royal ball, Violet woke up feeling as if she'd swallowed a beehive. Maggie tried to get her to eat, but the young girl wanted nothing to do with food.

"What's wrong, lass?" Maggie asked as Violet sat up in bed.

As much as she wished she could tell Maggie of her plans to escape, she thought it best to keep it a secret, for she didn't want to put the kind woman at risk.

So she simply said, "Not sure that I know."

Maggie reached over and felt the girl's forehead. "You're not warm to the touch. It's most likely nerves, dear. Your big day is finally here. The queen has asked you to stay in your room until it is time to announce you. What can I bring you to help pass the time? Would you like me to read you a story? Or perhaps you'd like to work on your needlework? I see it is coming along nicely."

Violet simply shrugged, hoping Maggie would leave her be. That was what she wanted more than anything, for she couldn't carry out her plans with the maidservant milling about.

Maggie smiled and said, "Well, I was going to wait until later, but I think it best that I show you now. Seems as though you need something to lift your spirits. Let me fetch your gown. The seamstress finished it late last night."

It took only a minute for her to make her way to the back of the room and around the corner where Violet's clothes were kept. She returned with a dress like nothing Violet had ever seen. It was a deep, rich purple, with delicate lace at the ends of the sleeves and a fashionable high collar.

"What do you think?" Maggie asked, smiling as if she held a chest filled with treasures. "The color certainly suits you. 'Tis stunning, eh?"

"I suppose," Violet said.

Maggie laughed. "I suppose? Is that the best you can do, now? You are going to look magnificent tonight, Violet."

"The queen doesn't think so," Violet said.

"I still can't figure out why you did it," Maggie said. "When you went to bed that night, your hair was fine. The next morning, I come in, and I find you practically bald."

"As I've told you, Maggie, I had my reasons, and it's best if I keep them to myself for now."

"May I ask what you did with your beautiful hair?" Maggie inquired. "When the queen scolded me for what you'd done, she asked me that very question. I told her I hadn't seen a trace of it."

Of course the queen would like to know what she'd done with the hair, so she might salvage a strand for her spell. Well, Violet had made certain she would never find it. Violet raised her chin and proudly responded, "I disposed of it in the horse stables. You don't want me to say more than that. Trust me."

Maggie wrinkled her nose. "Oh, heavens."

It made Violet smile, for a moment anyway, before her thoughts returned to the task at hand: getting out of the castle.

Maggie studied the girl for a good, long while. Finally, she spoke, her voice soft and soothing. "Yesterday, I thought it was your fate to go from tower to tiara. Looking at you now, seeing something in your eyes I've never seen before, I am no longer certain. Whatever it is that's going on, my love is with you, sweet Violet, and I am on your side. Always. Would you like some time alone, lass?"

Does she suspect? Violet wondered. *Does she suspect my plans for today?*

"I would indeed," Violet said. "Thank you."

After Maggie left, Violet got out of bed and pulled

out the pile of clothes Harry had snuck in for her. Her plan was simple. She would dress as a kitchen boy, and she would leave this place once and for all. But when she put on the trousers, they were much too large. And the drab tunic practically hung to the floor. Harry obviously hadn't checked the sizing. With a groan of frustration, Violet took off the clothing and tossed it aside. She scurried to the wardrobe, grabbed the simplest dress she could find, and slipped it on. It wasn't ideal, but it would have to do. If one of the servants questioned her, she'd simply say she was in need of some fresh air.

With that out of the way, she reached into her bed and grabbed the pirate figurine. She wanted to take it with her, for it would remind her to be strong and brave if the seas got rough. Of course, she hoped her escape would be smooth sailing, but there was no guarantee. In order to have her hands free, she tucked the figurine into her sash.

As she turned to go, something out the window

caught her eye. She moved closer to get a better look. What a strange sight, like nothing she'd ever seen before.

A long line of color flew through the air. It went to the center of the garden and became a circle. A living, breathing circle. It took Violet a moment to realize what it was. But then she knew, and at the realization, she couldn't help but smile. The birds had returned, joined by their friends, the butterflies, the bees, the dragonflies, and more. She'd never seen them fly in a circular fashion. It was almost as if they were in danger. Or trying to send a message.

Before Violet left, she quickly scanned the chamber, for she knew she would never return. She'd either become a minstrel, happy and free, or be caught and sent to the dungeon. Her resolve only grew stronger at the thought—she could not fail.

When her eyes landed on the harp, it pained her to think of leaving it behind. The instrument had been like a friend, soothing her nerves when she missed her mother desperately. She went to it and, soft as a breeze, strummed the lovely strings. Hopefully, if all went well, soon she would be traveling the world with her family, making beautiful music with them.

A candle sat by her bedside, which she took and

lit, using the fire burning in the hearth. Then, with candle in hand, she peeked outside her room. No one was coming, so like a mouse, she scurried down the hall and returned to the hidden door Harry had shown her. Fortunately, she slipped into the secret room without making a sound.

It took a while, as the passageway did indeed twist and turn, just as Harry had said. But eventually, she found herself in a small room, similar to the one she had entered. She set the candle on the shelf in the corner, which appeared to be there for that very purpose, and hurried out the door and into the fresh air and sunshine.

People were rushing about, all over the grounds, for there was much to be done on a day such as this. Fortunately, everyone was so busy that no one gave Violet a second look.

33

When Nuri awoke that morning, she lay there quietly, listening to the birds chirping in the nearby trees while she thought of her daughter back at the castle. She knew the day would be full of preparations for Violet. Preparations to make her the most beautiful princess in all the land.

What did her dress look like? Nuri wondered. How would they do her hair? Would she be given a crown to wear? How she longed to be there so she could witness it all.

Eventually, she forced herself to get up and take a bath in the rain barrel she'd found in the back of the property. After a meal of some bread and an apple, she made her way to the road, toward the market square.

She hadn't walked far when she heard feet pounding the dirt road behind her. The noise caused her to turn, curious as to who was coming and if someone perhaps needed help.

It was a boy running toward her. A boy with a crooked nose, wearing a dirty tunic.

Only a few other people were on the road, as it was late in the morning and most were already at the market square. No one else bothered to offer to help the boy. No one except Nuri.

"What is it, lad?" Nuri asked when he approached. "What's wrong? May I help you?"

The boy stopped and stared at the woman, his breathing hard and fast. "I'm wondering, by the look of your clothes and the tambourine in your basket, do you happen to be a minstrel?" he managed to ask in between breaths.

"Aye," she said.

He held his hand to his chest, as his breathing slowed slightly. "Do you know a woman named Nuri?"

"Of course," she said, curious as to why the boy would be looking for her. "That is I."

The boy smiled. "It is my lucky day. And yours, too! Hurry, you must come with me."

"Who are you?" she asked.

"I am Harry, a friend of Violet's. Your daughter is planning to escape today. Not only that, I saw a group of minstrels at the front of the castle this morning. Perhaps it is your family, looking for you and Violet."

Nuri wanted to ask a hundred questions, but she knew the best thing was to get to the castle as quickly as possible. She grabbed her skirts into her hands and began to run alongside the boy.

They ran past the chicken coop.

They ran past farms where cows grazed in the field.

They ran past folks who waved and called out to them, offering their assistance. Harry simply called back, "Do not worry, all is well," as necessary.

A while later, when the two approached the gates where the group of minstrels stood, Nuri slowed to a walk to catch her breath, and Harry followed suit. It didn't seem real. Was it truly them, after all this time?

As Nuri and Harry walked toward the group, the minstrels grew very quiet. Nuri's eyes filled with tears of joy, and her hands began to shake. She dropped everything and ran toward her family.

For a moment, it was total chaos as they reached for her, wanting to touch her as if to make sure she wasn't simply a figment of their imagination.

Her eyes searched and searched. Where was he? Why wasn't he here, the first to greet her? She pushed herself away, toward where the guard stood, and that's when she saw him. He stood there, watching from a distance, like a spectator trying to make sense of a new game. She wanted to go to him. To tell him how much she'd missed him and ask him why he hadn't come for them like he'd promised.

But something was wrong. She could sense it.

Something was horribly wrong with Marko.

34

*W*hen the girl the birds loved came out to greet them, there was so much that was different.

Her hair was different.

Her clothes were different.

Even the garden was different, for the one they'd known was gone.

But none of that mattered because the young girl had the same smile, the same lavender eyes, and the same love for them she'd always had.

"Oh, my dear ones, I've missed you. I've missed you so," Violet said from the middle of the circle, as she looked up at them flying around her. "We must leave this place, for it isn't safe. Perhaps the queen can take away our special garden, but she will never take away our special bond."

"Don't be so sure of that!" the queen called from behind Violet. "You listen, and you listen good. The birds are mine. The garden is mine. And for another year, until the hair on your head grows out, you are mine."

Peace and Pax watched as the queen approached the girl. Violet reached to her side and pulled something from her sash and held it tightly in her hand before she turned to face the queen.

"I am *not* yours, you evil witch. I will never be yours, for I am strong and brave, and I have love in my heart, unlike you. And these birds will not stay with the likes of you. You are selfish and mean, and they want nothing to do with you. Beauty will not make people or birds or anyone love you."

"Enough!" roared the queen. "I plan to take you to

the dungeon, where you will suffer greatly. You shall rue the day, young lady, that you cut your beautiful hair!"

Peace and Pax flew to Violet, wanting to help her somehow. But they were so small, and the queen so powerful.

As the two hummingbirds hovered in the air beside them, distracting the queen for a moment, one of Peace's feathers fell and fluttered through the air, toward the ground. Violet and the queen both lunged for it, but

the queen was a large woman and was not nimble like the small girl. The feather landed in Violet's hand while the queen tripped over herself and fell to the ground with a thud.

Violet took off running.

And the birds knew exactly what they must do next.

35

With the feather in one hand and the pirate figurine in the other, which she held to bring her luck, Violet ran toward the castle gates. She ran until she heard the gentle buzz of the insects and the birds grow louder and louder, and she wondered what was happening behind her.

When she turned to look, she could hardly believe her eyes. The birds and insects had swarmed the queen's face, her hair, her arms, her legs; they were everywhere, and it was all the queen could do to get back on her feet and run.

She ran, her arms flailing as she tried to escape the

swarming mass. But the creatures stuck together and did not let up.

They went toward the east end of the castle.

Violet watched as they chased the queen right toward the tower.

36

Nuri searched Marko's eyes. The recognition that should have been there was not. Nuri then understood that something had happened to him. That's why it'd taken so long for him to come for her.

As much as she wanted to help Marko, she couldn't fix everything at once.

"Violet needs us," Nuri said. "Harry, this boy here, has told me that Violet, our daughter, is trying to escape this day. Whatever feelings you do or do not have for me, please, will you help me get to her?"

"Of course," Marko said. "But the guard refuses to let us through. Even with offers of money."

Nuri approached the guard. "Let me ask you one question. Do you have a mother?"

The hard lines on his face softened as he replied, "I do not any longer. She died two seasons ago."

"Imagine her trying to get to you, and someone keeping you apart. That's what you're doing. My daughter needs us. Please, I beg you. If the queen discovers us, we swear on our daughter's life we will not implicate you. You will never be mentioned, mark my words."

He looked around and then put his lance back in its sheath. "I will let you through. But hurry. You do not have long."

The minstrels were following Harry past the gate when a voice sang out.

A voice Nuri would have recognized in a crowd of a thousand.

A strong voice who would commandeer a mattress turned ship.

A sweet voice who spoke of seeing her father and being free.

We don't know where we're going,
only know where we have been.
The road we're on is called Freedom,
and we'll walk it again and again.

Nuri, Marko, and the other minstrels watched as Violet came from around the corner, following the butterflies, the bees, and the birds, one after the other after the other, in a long string of glory.

Not impossibly small.

Magnificently immeasurable.

Nuri couldn't run to greet her fast enough.

"Mama," Violet squealed as Nuri knelt and let her daughter fall into her.

"My princess," Nuri whispered. "Oh, how I've missed you."

"I am glad to not be any princess but yours," Violet told her mother.

They held each other for a long time. When Nuri

reached up and rubbed Violet's bare head, they both giggled.

"What do you think of it?" Violet asked.

Nuri took the figurine from her daughter's hand. "Whether you are a princess or a pirate or a simple girl who loves birds, I think you look strong and brave. Just like your papa, who is here to finally meet you."

Marko took his cue and approached slowly. He extended his hand out for her to take. She still held the hummingbird's feather. "Hello, Papa," she said. "I am so happy to see you. Look here, I have a feather from one of my flying friends. They've rescued me from the evil queen."

Violet placed the feather in her father's outstretched hand, and like magic, the vacant look in his eyes disappeared. He took her hand and kissed it. "At last we finally meet, my dear daughter." Then he turned to Nuri, beaming. "I can remember. Thank heavens, my memory has returned."

"I never lost hope," Nuri said as Marko reached over and kissed his wife's cheek. "Can you recall what happened to you?"

"The queen cast a spell on me," Marko explained. "It took the feather of a hummingbird to break the curse." He swept Violet into his arms and spun her around, until they finally fell to the ground, both of them laughing. "You clever girl, you broke the curse!"

"I think you are the clever one," Violet said as she ran her finger along his jaw. "I've heard stories about you."

"Have you now?" he asked with a smile. "Do you have a favorite?"

"Yes," Violet replied, with a twinkle in her eye. "The story of the day you met your daughter is definitely my favorite."

37

*P*eace and Pax watched as the girl from the tower ran to greet her parents. They knew with certainty that love and freedom would be hers from now on.

They had chased the queen when she began to run. They chased her through the doorway of the tower and up a long spiral staircase and into a room. The queen had quickly shut the door, locking herself away from every creature, big and small, that she'd ever tried to make love her through spells or threats or demands. Satisfied, the birds, the bees, and the butterflies returned to join Violet and led her out of the garden to find her parents.

News of the day's events quickly spread, and Maggie and George rushed down to celebrate Violet's reunion with her family.

As Maggie stood there, tears filling her eyes, a brilliant blue butterfly flew up to greet her. Maggie held her finger out, as if to say *rest here and say hello*. The lovely butterfly accepted her offering and landed on her finger. Finally, with the elusive touch of a butterfly, the last of the witch's spells were broken.

George and Maggie had been two innocent victims of the queen's evil ways. Now they were transformed from their roles of gardener and maidservant to their true roles of king and queen.

Violet gasped when she saw Maggie in a royal blue gown and George with a plush red cape lined with white fur. They both wore jeweled crowns atop their heads.

Nuri and Violet curtsied. "Why didn't you tell us, Your Royal Highnesses?" Violet asked as she rose to her feet.

"Because I couldn't recall our true identities while under the spell," Maggie replied. "In fact, the entire kingdom was enchanted."

"It was extremely powerful," George said. "But thanks to Violet's feathered friends, who brought the rare indigo butterfly here today, we are finally free."

Maggie and George weren't the only ones affected. King Louis now stood before them wearing plain clothes, looking quite ashamed of himself.

"I assure you," he told Maggie and George and the others, "I played no part in any of this. I was as much a victim as the rest of you. If you'll remember, I was a tailor twenty years ago, before the witch cast her evil spell. It was at the special meeting, in the great hall." He looked at George. "Do you remember that day?"

"I do now," George replied. "A woman came to the castle and said she had vital information about a deadly virus making its way through the land. When I asked her to give me the information, she told me to assemble the masses so she could be sure all were well informed."

"It was the witch?" Violet asked.

Maggie nodded. "The witch cast her horrible spell on us that day. But all is well now, thanks to you, Violet. Marko and Nuri, will you stay on at the castle? We'd love for you to, in whatever capacity you'd like."

"I'm afraid we are wandering minstrels at heart," Nuri said. "We look forward to showing our daughter the life she has missed out on for so long."

"Will I play music with you, Mama?" Violet asked. "While I was training to be a princess, I learned to play the harp."

"Aye, my daughter," Nuri replied. "You will never have a day without music. I promise you that." She turned and spoke to Maggie and George. "But please do not worry. We will return often to visit."

"You are welcome anytime," George replied. "Please, consider this your home."

Violet turned to her friend Harry. "I shall miss you. Thank you for all you have done to help me."

He gave her a sad smile. "I shall miss you as well, but I'm glad freedom is finally yours."

"Some of the birds will follow us, but I suspect some shall want to stay here, in the beautiful gardens," Violet said. "Would you keep them company from time to time?"

"I would be delighted to," Harry replied.

George turned and spoke to Harry. "It would please me greatly to appoint you the new gardener of the castle. I'm happy to teach you everything I know. Of course, our first task shall be to return the secret garden to its original state."

Harry's eyes lit up. Violet laughed and gave her friend's arm a happy squeeze. Harry bowed. "It will be my honor, Your Majesty, to care for the beautiful gardens."

"Good!" the king said. "Then it is done."

The crowd buzzed with excitement over all the good news.

"Wait," Marko said, shaking his head, as if he'd just had a revelation. "I've recalled the specific spell the queen cast on me—'Only the feather of a humming-bird will free your mind, grant your wish.' So I believe I have one wish to make. What shall I wish for?"

Violet was the first to speak. "Do not wish for fine clothes or good food. Do not wish for a feather bed or a warm fire. And most of all, do not wish for beauty, as the queen did, for none of those will bring you true happiness."

"Tell me, my wise daughter. What would you have me wish for?"

"That anyone who sets eyes on a hummingbird will find joy in its magnificence, now and forever."

"There is nothing else you want?" her father asked with surprise in his voice.

"My wish has already come true," Violet said. "I

drew a picture of it one day in the tower. Remember, Mama? I drew the three of us smiling, because we were thankful to be free."

"Ah," Marko said. "Of course it has. Then your wish for the hummingbirds is mine as well."

"We should have a party," Violet said, looking at the king and queen. "To celebrate this day. Why, I even have a pretty purple dress I can wear."

"What a fine idea," King George said. He clapped his hands loudly twice. "The royal ball will go on as planned. Please, back to your preparations, everyone."

"But I shall not be crowned princess," Violet said as she turned toward the castle with her mother and father on either side of her. "I just want to be a young minstrel." She paused for a moment. "Except, of course, on the days I want to be a pirate."